THE

GASLIGHT

KNIGHTS

(ANOTHER SHADE OF GRAY SEQUEL)

J.L. FREDRICK

First Edition

ISBN: 0615747205
ISBN-13: 978-0615747200

Cover design by Lovstad Publishing

For Doug

More Novels by J.L. Fredrick

Thunder in the Night
The Great Train Robbery of Monroe County
Mad City Bust
September Ten
Aftermath
Cursed by the Wind
Another Shade of Gray
Across the Dead Line
The Other End of the Tunnel

Non-Fiction
Rivers, Roads, and Rails

ACKNOWLEDGMENTS

My personal recollection of the *Stoddard Hotel*
when I often went there with friends for lunch
while attending college in La Crosse.

Associate Archives Librarian Bill Petersen
at the La Crosse Public Library for his wonderful
help in researching more time period elements
and providing some excellent vintage photos
of the *Stoddard Hotel.*

My good friend and fellow author Alan Douglas
for his faithful attention, feedback, and constructive
critiques of this story all during its creation.
Thanks, Buddy!

THE
GASLIGHT
KNIGHTS

CHAPTER ONE

THE night they pulled Johnny Dempsey's body out of the Mississippi River is when Andy and I, Will Madison, decided to get out of town while the gettin' was good, no matter what it took. We hadn't known Johnny a long time, but long enough. That went for some of his other friends, too. At one time we thought they were all a bunch of great guys, but as the weeks and months passed by, it became clear to us that we had jumped off a perfectly good boat into a cesspool of trouble. If we hadn't been using our heads, we might've gotten tangled in a mess we didn't want.

And speaking of perfectly good boats, that's why Andy and I were in the middle of that mess. We had had three good seasons aboard the Madison, an elegant old lady of a steamboat, of which I was a part owner, with my big brother Jesse Madison and our good friend Luke Jackson. We'd owned that old boat for six years, and she made us a good living hauling rich folks up and down the Mississippi on vacation excursions. Oh, we had our share of headaches, too, but for the most part, we had it better than most people, considering the Depression and all that went with it. And then one night while we were tied up at the St. Louis levee, a fire broke out on the boat next to the Madison. That fire spread so rapidly that by the time anybody could do anything it had raged across five more boats. The Madison was a total loss.

Jesse, Luke, and I came out of it okay. All the staff was off duty between excursions so nobody was injured. The insurance company paid us off, but we were all out of work kinda sudden like. Wasn't long, though, until Jesse got hooked up with the captain of a barge tow—the Bill Horne—he and Luke signed on with the condition that once they had a little experience with pushing barges, they would be in line for Captain and Pilot of the next available boat in the company.

Barge tows don't have pianos or piano players, so Andy was officially an unemployed piano player, and Jesse told me that as soon as he became the captain of another boat, I would be back on the river again. And if Andrew was willing to work as a deckhand, he'd have a job, too. So, in the meantime, Andy and I went back to St. Charles with his mom, Beth Lorado, who was one of our chambermaids, to their house at the end of Third Street, where I had spent the winter when Andy and I first met. Andy's dad, Marion Lorado, who was one of our engineers, was already hired as the second engineer on another barge tug, so we didn't see much of him. Beth went back to teaching piano lessons, and Mildred, the other chambermaid on the Madison, got Beth a part-time job at the hotel where she worked.

Luke was our pilot. He could afford most anything he wanted, and he made sure Reggie had a nice place to live in St. Louis until he could get him back on a riverboat crew again. Reggie had eventually become the Captain's First Mate after he worked as a deckhand for a while. He and Luke, of course, had been sharing quarters since our first day on the river aboard the Madison. We all learned in time what was going on between them, but it didn't seem to bother anybody, so it really didn't matter.

So everything worked out alright for all of us.

Andy was the best piano player I'd ever heard tickle the ivories. He played the church organ in St. Charles, too. That's how I happened to first meet Andy. I'd seen him many times before, and I had thought that he was a homeless kid without good clothes or food. But then I saw him playing the church organ, and I finally got to meet him—well, he actually found me lost in the woods one day and he showed me the way back to town. After that, we got to be really good friends, and I lived with his family while the Madison was tied up in Alton Slough one winter. That's when the Madison was remodeled into a luxury excursion boat, and Jesse hired Andy as cabin boy and the live entertainment. He hired Andy's mom and dad, too, as chambermaid and second engineer.

We called him *Andrew* back then, and he was a bit shy about performing in front of all those people, but after about a year or so, "Andy" Lorado had become quite popular with the vacationers, and some of them came back for another trip... "Just to hear Andy play their favorite tunes." On every trip, at least once or twice, Andy would always get me to the piano to play a duet with him. I couldn't play the piano except to pick out a melody, *Down by the Riverside*, with one finger, and   Andy would play a dreamy rendition of *April in Paris* at the same time, and somehow he could make me sound like a real professional. Of course, we always hammed it up a bit, too. It never failed to bring the house down. He taught me some more tunes later on, and eventually we played together more often, but I knew it was Andy that the crowd loved.

Ever since I ran away from home in Milwaukee to escape the daily beatings by my usually drunken stepfather, I had learned to hate the big city. I was only fourteen then, when I jumped a freight train headed west and landed someplace near a big river. I had no idea where I was or what to do next, but I managed to learn how to take care of myself, stealing clothes off a line in a back yard when I needed some, and swiping a loaf of bread cooling on a back porch, and raiding gardens late at night. I found places to sleep in haylofts, and in general, I was getting along pretty good. But it was lonely.

Then one night a bad storm hit—took the roof off the barn I was sleeping in! I ran into the woods so I wouldn't be found and stayed the rest of the night in a little cave. By then I had wandered so far I wasn't sure if I was still in the same country. The next morning a flood filled the valley because of all the heavy rain the night before, and as I sat there watching it, I noticed a young man chasing after something floating away in the floodwater. I saw the top of a trunk coming toward me and when I thought I could grab it for him, I went head-first into the swift, muddy stream, too. Guess I would've drowned if Jesse Madison hadn't found me and pulled me out. Now Jesse could've hauled me right to the nearest police station and turned me in for the runaway that I was. But he didn't. Guess he felt sorry for me. He even lied to the clerk when he bought me some new clothes—said I was his "little brother," I guess so nobody would ask any questions. He sort of took me in, and it wasn't long until I changed my last name to Madison, and Jesse and I *were* brothers. It was the greatest thing that ever happened to me.

Jesse met a lady friend on our first trip down the river on

our new boat. Oh, yeah... the boat. Another guy, Luke Jackson, had joined up with us, and we met an old riverboat captain named Augie on the riverfront at La Crosse. He owned the boat, and he invited us aboard to take a look. We became good friends with Augie, and he let us stay there for a while. But old Augie was sort of down on his luck, and he lost the boat in a poker game one night. We felt awful. Jesse, Luke, and I had planned to work as crewmen for Augie on his boat.

Just about the time we thought all was lost, along came Spades Morgan struttin' off another steamboat that came in from St. Paul. Jesse and I had met him before, up in Alma, and we knew he was a professional gambler. He was a great guy, though, but we didn't know how important he would become to us. He agreed to help us get Augie's boat back from the swamp scum gambler J.D. McDermott. He did win it back, but by then Augie had decided to retire, and he didn't want it. That's how Jesse became its official owner, and of course, later on, he made me and Luke partners. Luckily, Augie consented to stay with us as the pilot for a while and teach us all how to run a riverboat. He was a good teacher. Luke learned piloting and a year or so later, he got his pilot's license. Jesse became a first-class Captain and entrepreneur. And I was the most popular cabin boy on the river.

Sadly, though, we laid Augie to rest in St. Charles the next year when he died of a heart attack. But I think he died a happy man.

Like I started before, the lady friend Jesse met, Sadie Perkins, eventually became his wife and the mother of their son, Philip. Sadie was a top-notch photographer, and just moving to St. Louis where she was starting a photography and art studio. She booked passage on our boat from La Crosse to St. Louis, and it must've been love at first sight for her and Jesse, because they spent the first night in a hotel while the boat was tied up overnight at Prairie du Chien.

They had to part when we reached St. Louis, and it was more than two years later when Jesse found her again; Philip was almost two. They married and lived in Sadie's house in St. Louis.

They invited me to stay with them, too. But I hated the big city—any big city—and St. Louis was a *very* big city. That's why I chose to stay in St. Charles with Andrew's family that next winter.

As time went on, though, I visited them more often and stayed there frequently when the boat was not busy or was in harbor for repairs. Gradually, I disliked the city less and learned to tolerate the rows of tall buildings towering over my head, and the noisy traffic and pedestrians at ground level. I learned my way around, although I didn't bother trying to remember street names, just familiar buildings and other things at the corners. I had learned my lesson about getting lost out in the woods, and so I paid closer attention to landmarks starting the very first time I decided to explore the streets of St. Louis.

CHAPTER TWO

WHEN the Madison burned in September of 1934, my world sort of turned upside down, as I'm sure it did for the others, too. One thing I could be thankful for was that Big Brother Jesse had always insisted that we keep all of our valuables and money in the safe instead of hiding it in our cabins. That safe must've weighed a ton and the walls and door were a foot thick. When we finally found the safe and got it opened the day after the fire, everything was still intact; we hadn't lost a thing. All the important business papers and books were unharmed, and just about everyone on the staff retrieved their canvas bags containing personal valuables and money. A gold pocket watch that Spades Morgan gave me five years ago and about eight hundred dollars were in my bag. I think I hugged Jesse and kissed him on the cheek for always making me keep it there. Even Andy hugged Jesse out of pure joy when he got out the bag with his name on it. All that helped ease the pain of seeing our beloved boat, the Madison, lying there in a charred heap of rubble. A salvage company towed away the hull, said they would try to save some of the machinery and boilers, but the rest was simply worthless junk.

Captain Brooks from the towboat Bill Horne was there when Jesse, Luke and I watched the salvage tug haul away what remained of the Madison. He knew Jesse and Luke, as many of the riverboat captains and pilots were acquainted. He shook our hands, offered his sympathy. And then he offered Jesse and Luke jobs on his boat. "Once you get a little experience towin' barges," he said, "Continental will put you in command of one of their other boats."

It didn't take Jesse long to accept the offer, and Luke seemed pretty excited about it, too. They all shook hands again, after they had set a time later that day for an official meeting at the Continental Shipping Company's office, and then Captain Brooks left.

Jesse looked up and down the levee, and then he looked at me. "Will, as soon as I'm on another boat of my own, you'll be there on my crew... I promise."

Tears were burning my eyes, and I wasn't sure if they were tears of joy for Jesse, or tears of sorrow that we wouldn't be together for quite some time. "What about Andy?" I said, for the lack of anything better to say.

"I really like Andy," Jesse replied. "If he's willing to work as a deckhand, or maybe a cook's assistant, you can tell him he has a job waiting for him, too."

"Yeah," I said. "I guess barge tows don't need a piano player, do they?"

We all laughed a little. At least, I had *something* to look forward to. "I think I'll go with Andy and Beth back to St. Charles this afternoon. Mildred is going, too. She checked the bus schedules. There's one at three fifteen.

"You know, Will, you can stay with me and Sadie."

"I know. But Andy's a little down in the dumps about all this, and I think he could use a little company for a while."

"Guess that's a good enough reason to go to St. Charles. But just remember... you can come to our house anytime."

He gave me one of those sincere Big Brother bear hugs that had never lost their effectiveness. I returned the gesture, thinking about all the good times we had, and all the good things Jesse had done for me. I had a lot of faith in my big brother, and I knew he'd never let me down. I detected tears in his eyes, too, but I wasn't sure if they were tears for me, or for the boat. I wanted to think they were for me.

The bus to St. Charles was late. It was nearly five o'clock when it left the St. Louis station, and quite crowded. Beth and Mildred found seats across the aisle from each other near the front, but Andy and I had to share the seat across the back of the bus with an old couple who could barely keep awake. The old man kept tipping over onto me, and he'd wake up when I pushed him back. "Oh, excuse me," he'd say every time. "Guess I must've dozed off."

At least it kept Andy amused. It was the first time I had seen him smile all day.

We arrived in St. Charles a little after six. I hugged Mildred when Andy and I finally struggled our way through the crowd gathered to meet other disembarking passengers. Mildred seemed so worried, but I sensed that she was more worried about me than she was about herself. "Everything will be okay," she said to me. "You just keep smiling, and everything will turn out just fine."

"Will you be okay?" I asked her. I knew she was headed off to her little apartment downtown, and she would be alone.

"Oh, heavens, yes! Don't you worry about me. I'll be just fine."

I didn't worry about her, but I *was* concerned. Mildred was like a mom to me. She had seen me through my adolescence, and I knew she truly cared about me. I loved her very dearly.

"We'll be in touch," she said, and then she pushed me away from our embrace, turned, and briskly strutted down the side-walk toward Main Street.

"Stop over for coffee tomorrow if you can," Beth called out to her.

Mildred turned and waved. "Thank you. I will."

Beth, Andy, and I walked casually out to their house at the end of Third Street. Beth had already been home a couple of days after the last excursion, and she had just left there that morning on the bus back to St. Louis when she got word about the Madison fire. Her husband, Marion, had stayed in St. Louis to help with some maintenance on the boat, and Andy decided to stay there with me, so she had come alone. When she unlocked the back door into the kitchen, I could tell she was glad to be home again. "I'll make a pot of coffee, and then we'll have some supper," she said.

As we sat at the kitchen table eating the pancakes and bacon that Andy suggested, Beth asked: "What are your plans, now, Will? You'll need some new clothes, won't you?"

"I guess so," I replied. "I have a few things at Jesse's place, but I s'pose I'll be needing some more."

"And what would you like for your birthday supper next week?"

I had almost forgotten. Next week, Monday, the 24th of September was my eighteenth birthday. It was just like Beth Lorado to remember. "Oh, you don't have to bother," I said modestly.

"It's no bother. I have to make supper anyway, and you can make your request."

I thought for a long moment. "Well... how 'bout biscuits and your delicious chicken stew?"

"If that's what you want, that's what you'll get."

Andy piped up. "Can you bake a cake, too?"

"Sure," Beth replied with a big smile. "We can have cake, too."

It was a pretty fantastic birthday, considering the catastrophic turn of events that preceded it. The Madison's destruction was still quite heavy on everybody's thoughts, but that didn't stop Jesse, Luke, Reggie, and Mildred from showing up Monday afternoon for the best birthday party ever. They all carried in brightly wrapped packages and Jesse had a tub of strawberry ice cream—he knew how I loved ice cream.

When the day was over, I no longer had a clothing shortage problem, as all the packages contained shirts, trousers, and Luke and Reggie gave me socks and underwear. But Jesse didn't have a package; instead, he handed me a paper envelope. When I opened it and looked inside, I couldn't believe my eyes. Baseball tickets. In just a few days the St. Louis Cardinals and the Detroit Tigers would face off for the 1934 World Series, and I had two tickets for the games that would be played in St. Louis. "Didn't want you to go alone," Jesse said, "so I got tickets for Andy, too."

Jesse was the greatest.

CHAPTER THREE

IT was the middle of October. I was getting restless, and so was Andy. We'd taken a bus to St. Louis and watched Dizzy Dean and the "Gashouse Gang" Cardinals whip the Detroit Tigers, and listened to the radio broadcast from Detroit of the last game of the Series when they massacred the Tigers eleven to nothing. Now the excitement was over. Beth was teaching piano lessons to less-than-talented little kids again, and Mildred had coaxed her into a part-time job at the hotel where she worked. Andy practiced at the piano every day, and I read a lot of books when we weren't trying to escape the painful renditions of *Twinkle, Twinkle Little Star* and *Mary Had a Little Lamb* from Beth's students.

Then one day the telephone rang, and when Beth told me it was Sadie calling for me, I thought for sure that Jesse was ready to get me and Andy on a riverboat crew.

"Hello?" I spoke with enthusiasm.

"Will?" Sadie sounded tired or distressed, I couldn't tell which.

"How are you doing, Will?"

"Good, Sadie. How are you?"

"I'm okay, but I was wondering if you could come to St. Louis and stay here for a while. My babysitter has fallen and broken her leg, and Philip just doesn't like any of the others I can get on such short notice. I'm really busy in the studio these days, and I sure could use your help. Philip would love to see you again, too."

"Well, I s'pose. Where's Jesse?"

"Jesse is on the way to New Orleans. I don't expect him back for at least two weeks."

"New Orleans! Well, that lucky son of a gun."

"How about it, Will? Can you come?"

"Sure, Sadie. I'll see what time the bus goes tomorrow, okay?"

"Okay! That would be great! I'll see you tomorrow, then."

"Okay. Good-bye Sadie."

"Good-bye Will."

In a way, I was glad to have a change of scenery, but I also hated to leave Andy all alone with just his piano and having to dodge the Twinkle, Twinkle kids all by himself. Then it occurred to me that Andy could come to St. Louis with me.

"Sadie has a piano in her parlor," I told Andy. "You can still practice every day if you want to."

"But where will I sleep?"

"There's a big double bed in my room."

"How do you know it's okay with Sadie?"

"I'll call her back right now."

I knew Sadie wouldn't say no. She needed my help, and she knew how close me and Andy were. And besides... she liked Andy, and Philip adored him. It would be perfect.

"Of course, Andy can come with you," Sadie said. "It'll be good for both of you."

When I knew Andy was convinced that he should come to St. Louis with me, Beth was my next obstacle. But she wasn't as difficult to persuade as I had expected. She was actually glad that Andy wanted to get out and explore his options. "As long as he's going with you, Will," she said, "I shouldn't have to worry at all. And I know you'll both be in good hands with Sadie."

Beth loaned us a spare satchel to put our clothes in; both Andy's and mine were lost in the fire. We jumped on the bus to St. Louis the next morning.

Jesse and Sadie's house on Fulton Street hadn't changed much in all the time I had been going there. It was a quite large two story Victorian style, painted white with blue trim, just like the Madison had been. Even Andy remarked about the resemblance when he saw it. The huge front parlor had been converted into the business end of Sadie's studio; one side was partitioned off with floor-to-ceiling drapes that parted in the middle, behind which were cameras on tripods, chairs, and several different backdrop screens. This is where close-up portrait photographs were taken. In the far corner on the other side stood a dressing table and mirror, where the women could apply make-up and restore hair-dos that might have been disturbed by the wind. Plenty of comfortable chairs offered a congenial atmosphere among several easels holding paintings and photographs that aptly displayed Sadie's talents. Right in the center sat a large desk where Sadie conducted business.

Sadie was happy to see us when we came in the front door. She sat at her desk, busy with a stack of paperwork, and 3½-year-old Philip was busy beside her on the floor with a pile of wooden building blocks. His blue stuffed rabbit, "Abba," that I had given to him for Christmas a couple of years before, wasn't far away.

"Hi, Will. Hi Andy," Sadie said with her usual smile. "It's so good to see you again."

I hadn't seen Sadie since before the fire. I gave her a hug when she got up from behind the desk. Philip left his blocks and came running. I scooped him up and he hugged my neck. Then he noticed Andy. "Doo!" he squealed, and reached out for Andy's turn to be coddled and hugged. Philip had called Andy "Doo" when he first started talking, because he couldn't pronounce "Andrew." The name just stuck. He liked Andy as much as he liked me, and he seemed pretty excited to have us both there.

Sadie glanced at the clock. "Some customers will be here soon," she said. "You can take your things upstairs... and there are some fresh cookies just out of the oven in the kitchen if you're hungry."

With Philip riding on Andy's shoulders and clutching Abba, they followed me up the stairs to the bedroom where I always slept when I stayed there. I was so glad to see that Sadie had been thoughtful enough to replace the pink-and-white bedspread with a blue one.

While Sadie conducted usual business with several clients throughout the afternoon, Andy and I kept Philip amused until he tired, ready for a long nap. That routine lasted all week while we took turns playing with Philip, and Andy spent about an hour each day at the piano in Sadie's parlor. Sometimes he'd coax me to the piano bench so we could play our *"Down by the Riverside/April in Paris"* duet. Whenever I had the chance, I spent time in the studio with Sadie when she wasn't busy with customers, and I suppose she got tired of me asking all sorts of questions about cameras and picture-taking. But in a way, she seemed pleased, too, that I was taking an interest. When I asked her if I could try my hand at taking a picture, she opened a cupboard, pulled out a black case, and then took a small camera out of the case. "I've had this for three or four years," she told me, "but I hardly ever use it anymore." She turned it over, examining all sides, and then held it up to her eyes, panning around, viewing various portions of the room through the lens. Then she offered to let me hold it. "This is a thirty-five millimeter Leica... uses roll film, easy to operate. It would be a good camera for you to try," she said.

I took the camera from her with a little hesitation, fearful that I might damage it just by touching it.

"Don't be afraid of it, Will. It won't bite you."

Carefully, I imitated Sadie's earlier actions by holding it up to my eye and looking through the lens. I saw the world differently and I immediately became fascinated.

"This is the kind of camera that a lot of newspaper and magazine journalists use," Sadie explained. "You can take it just about anywhere but underwater. I was thinking of giving journalism photography a try, but it's men that dominate all the newspaper and magazine photographer jobs so I decided to just stick with what I do."

I had seen hundreds of people vacationing aboard the Madison, and many of them carried cameras much like this one. Seemed like there was always someone taking pictures of the scenery along the Mississippi from our decks, and sometimes they would take pictures of their family, and occasionally they would take pictures of me and some of the rest of the crew. The pilothouse and Luke were always popular subjects, too.

Sadie retrieved from the black case a thin book and offered it to me. "Here... read this manual first so you understand a little more about it, and then tomorrow I'll help you load some film and you can take a few pictures. I'll develop the film for you, and we'll see how you did."

I studied that manual from cover to cover, several times. The next day while Philip was napping and Andy was practicing on the piano, Sadie gave me a crash course in photography—how to hold the camera and keep it steady, how to always try to keep the sun at my back and to avoid shadows, how to "compose" the subject in the viewfinder, and all sorts of other little tricks she had learned from experience. I absorbed as much as I could. She showed me how to put the film in; I was ready to take pictures.

Choosing the subjects to photograph was tough. I don't know why I wasted so much effort on making that decision; I would have many more opportunities. I finally decided on

Jesse's house, one of Andy, a couple of shiny new cars in the street, and various street scenes downtown. When I came back to the house, Sadie showed me how to remove the film safely, and said she would develop the pictures in a day or so.

I'd had plenty of time to think about what Sadie said about journalism photography, and I had really enjoyed seeking my subjects and composing the scene in the viewfinder. Hearing the click of the shutter made me feel like I had recorded a piece of time for all eternity. If Jesse wasn't successful in getting me back on the river soon, I thought I'd like to try this photography business.

CHAPTER FOUR

SATURDAY, Sadie must've felt sorry for us and told Andy and me to get out for a while and enjoy ourselves... maybe see a matinee. We hadn't done that for a long time, and it sounded like a good idea. There were several theaters to choose, and one of them was bound to be playing something we would like. We took a trolley car to Grand Boulevard and Olive Street, the center of the midtown theater district.

When we came out of the Fox movie theater that afternoon, we stood on the sidewalk next to Grand Boulevard for a while watching all the people scurrying by. We weren't looking for anyone in particular, or attempting to make any new acquaintances. That's when another young fellow who looked to be about our age casually walked up to us and said "Hi."

Andy and I acknowledged his greeting.

"Saw you goin' in the theater earlier," he said. "Thought I should know you from somewhere."

Andy and I exchanged glances and shrugged our shoulders. The handsome young face didn't seem familiar, but we had seen so many faces over the past few years, it was nearly impossible to remember them all.

"We were on a riverboat crew until a month ago," Andy offered. "The Madison. Were you ever on it?"

The stranger thought a long moment, and then shook his head. "No, but isn't that one of the boats that burned about a month ago?"

"That's right," Andy replied. "But if you were never on it, then I don't know why you think you know us."

"Well... maybe I've just seen you along the waterfront. I spend quite a bit of time there."

"What d'ya do there?" Andy asked.

"Write my poetry."

"You write poetry?" I blurted out, not intending to sound rude, but it may have seemed that way. I think I must've struck a sensitive nerve. "I'm sorry," I added. "I didn't mean it the way it sounded."

"That's okay," the stranger replied. "I'm getting used to that response from people." Then he stuck out his right hand toward Andy. "I'm Marty Genshaw."

Andy accepted his brief handshake, and then Marty offered the same to me.

"I'm Will Madison, and my friend is Andy Lorado."

Marty eyed me with suspicion. "Madison. Any relation to the boat?"

"Well... yeah... me and my brother Jesse owned it."

The breezy October air was getting just a little chilly as the sun dipped behind the tall buildings leaving us in the shadows. Marty wore only a T-shirt and jeans, and I could see the goose bumps flourishing on his arms. "There's a coffee shop just around the corner," I suggested. "We can get in out of this wind. I'll buy the coffee."

The others agreed and we all headed around the corner.

Marty asked a lot of questions about the Madison, and what it was like to work on a riverboat. He seemed to turn his interest mostly to Andy when he found out Andy was a musician. Watching people aboard the Madison, I had noticed that people of the arts tend to be attracted to one another.

"Have any of your poems been published?" Andy asked.

"No," Marty replied. "I'm kinda new at poetry. I switched from prose to poetry only about a year ago while I was..." His face turned strawberry red as he abruptly cut off.

"While you were... what?" Andy asked.

After a long pause staring down into his coffee cup, Marty hesitantly finished the statement. "Okay... I guess you would've found out sooner or later... while I was in jail."

"Why were you in jail?" I asked.

"For stealing a typewriter... but I was just borrowing it... I was going to bring it back... honest!"

"But you got caught taking it without permission, so you got thrown in the slammer for theft."

"Yeah, something like that."

I wasn't sure if I should believe he was truly sincere. Marty was a dynamo, a ball of energy with legs and arms, and probably a hustler for any kind of action. My first impulse was to beware. But Andy seemed quite comfortable with our new acquaintance.

"I quit school when I was sixteen and got a job as an office boy in a New York publishing house," Marty went on.

"You're from New York?" Andy asked.

"Yeah... and that's when I decided I wanted to be a writer." His eyes quickly jerked back and forth from Andy to me; his expression appeared as if he was concerned about losing our attention.

"Then, why did you come to St. Louis?" Andy said.

"After almost a year in prison, I just wanted to get away from New York. I'd educated myself quite well by reading *everything* in the prison library—that's when I became fond of poetry, and even started writing some. But when I was released, I met a man from St. Louis in a tea pad, there in New York. He told me about St. Louie, and so I decided to come here."

"Whoa! Whoa!" Andy said. "A tea… what?"

I was curious, too.

Marty looked at us like we must've been from another planet. "*Tea pad*… you know… like an opium den, where you can go to smoke marihuana and hashish. There's hundreds of 'em in New York. They're here in St. Louis, too."

We'd heard about marihuana and hashish becoming popular as substitutes for alcohol during prohibition days, but we'd never been exposed to it. Neither Andy nor I had spent enough time in the big city to be familiar with "tea pads." Marty explained that they were similar to the speakeasies of prohibition, where illegal booze was available, but only if you were a member of the "private club." But apparently, tea pads were more acceptable and not necessarily under scrutiny of the law.

I decided to ease up on my torrid feelings toward Marty, primarily because Andy really seemed to like him; if prison had rehabilitated him and turned him into an intellect, then I guess I couldn't think of any reason to dislike him.

While Andy and Marty conversed about music and poetry, I thought some more about the Leica camera and all the other things I would like to put into pictures. I certainly hoped that Sadie would let me use it again, or maybe even sell it to me. I'd go to the levee and wait for some really good riverboat scenes, and... and... maybe I'd see Marty there, and then I could show him that I was eligible to be called an "artist." But I decided right then that I wouldn't wait for that. "I'm learning photography," I said when the opportunity came. "Maybe I'll be a journalism photographer someday."

"Well," Marty said, as if he were finally accepting me into an exclusive group. "I have a friend who works at the *Post*. He's just a copy boy now, but he's studying to be a journalist, too. You should meet him sometime."

"Okay... sure," I said, hoping that I hadn't overstepped the boundaries. I knew scarcely little about photography, and I knew absolutely nothing about journalism. But it certainly couldn't hurt to meet Marty's friend.

I pulled out my pocket watch. It was nearly five o'clock. "We should be going," I said to Andy. "Sadie will be waiting supper on us."

We agreed to meet Marty again the following Friday night. He'd take us to a place called the Lion's Den, a bar at North Sixth and Olive Street. That was only about three blocks from the river.

CHAPTER FIVE

ONLY half of the pictures I took with the *Leica* camera were worth keeping. Sadie explained the reasons—I didn't hold the camera steady, overexposed, underexposed—it was clear that I had a long way to go to become a good photographer, or even a mediocre one.

"Don't be discouraged," Sadie told me. "You actually did pretty good for your first try."

"You really think so, or are you just saying that to make me feel better?"

"Really. You did better than I did on my first try."

Whether it was the truth or not, it did make me feel better, and I wanted to try again. "Can I try some more? I'll pay you for the film and the developing."

"Sure, you can try some more, but you don't have to pay me for the film. I owe you that much for helping me take care of Philip."

Every day that week, I took more pictures, and Sadie helped me with a few of them to get the camera settings just right. The next picture I took of Andy turned out nice, but I thought he looked a lot younger in the picture. By Friday I had a collection of photographs, and even Sadie was impressed with some of them. "You'll make a good photographer, Will. You should keep at it."

Somehow, I knew this is what I wanted to do. I still loved the river, too, and I would go back to a riverboat in a heartbeat if Jesse offered. But photography would allow me to ex-press myself creatively, something that had not occurred to me until now. The whole idea of it was exciting. Andy gave me plenty of encouragement, too. "Some of your pictures are just as good as any in the newspaper," he said.

Now I wasn't afraid to meet Marty's friend and talk about photography. Of course, I still knew nothing about journal-ism, but I could learn that, too, with a little help.

Andy and I rode a bus again Friday night destined for the midtown theater district. Just as he said he would, Marty was there to meet us. We boarded a street car that went all the way down Olive Street toward the Mississippi River. We got off at 6th Street. I recognized the neighborhood, because just one block away—6th & Pine—there was a sandwich shop within walking distance from the St. Louis levee where Luke, Reggie and I used to go when the Madison tied up overnight. Andy had been with us a few times, too.

The crowd in the Lion's Den was rather subdued, mellow, when we arrived, but I guess that was because it was still ear-ly. As the night wore on, though, voices got bolder, the music played louder, and the beer flowed more freely. Marty led us to a table in the back corner area that was sectioned off from the main floor with a half-wall. From the top of the wall to the ceiling grew ivy vines on white painted lattice. Gas lights gently illuminated the room. Five more tables took up the secluded space where four of them were occupied by poker games. The partition was evidently there to provide a little protection from the crowd for such purposes. The table where Marty's friends sat seemed to be more of a social gath-ering with no gaming. They all greeted Marty, happy that he could join the party. And then they all took notice of me and Andy. "Who are your friends?" one of them asked. He didn't appear to be irritated with our intrusion, but instead, he seemed eager to have us join the party, too.

"Knights of the Square Table," Marty addressed the group. "I'd like you to meet Andy Lorado, unemployed musician." He put his arm across Andy's shoulders. "Andy was the entertainer on the steamboat Madison that burned a while back." Then he put his hand on my shoulder. "This is Will Madison, ex-steamboat owner. He's studying photography."

"Knights of the *Square* Table?" I chuckled.

Marty eyed me with pseudo seriousness. "Well... yeah... Knights of the *Round* Table was already taken."

Everyone sitting there laughed, and then Andy and I were invited to pull up chairs from the vacant table. They all shifted one way or the other to make a couple of open spaces.

At first, I got the impression that these guys were upper class in social circles; they all wore nice clothes, their speech was correct and polite, and they weren't loud or boisterous. I had been among a large number of high standards people on the Madison; those were the people we catered to—the wealthy businessmen and their families—and the young men sitting around this table, although they were much younger than most of our passengers had been, seemed to possess similar qualities.

As with almost any group, newcomers are always the center attraction. Marty had disappeared while the others were fussing over making Andy and me comfortable, but he soon returned with three glass beer mugs and a pitcher filled with golden brew topped with a mound of white foam. He poured the mugs full, slid one across the table to Andy and one to me, and then set the pitcher in the middle of the table where there was another one nearly empty. "I hope you like beer," he said. "Guess I should've asked first."

Andy and I both assured him his choice was okay, and we sampled the cold brew.

The guy sitting to my left offered a handshake. "I'm Curtis," he said. And then the guy sitting next to him reached across for a handshake. "I'm Frank."

I noticed that on the other side of the table Andy was receiving the same treatment. "They call me Cheechee," the fellow next to him said. "Real name is Christopher Chapman." He reached across the table to shake my hand, too, and that's when I took notice of his extremely good looks and that he seemed a little younger than the rest.

The others introduced themselves with handshakes, too; Leo Majors and Johnny Dempsey offered pleasant greetings. They seemed much older than the rest by at least four or five years.

I gathered from listening to the various conversations that evening that this circle of friends was much larger than what was present here; many of the "Knights" were aspiring writers; some of them were off to various parts of the country seeking education or employment, or in some cases pleasure, because they hadn't yet found their sense of direction. Someone by the name of Milo Lipinski was in New York trying to get into Columbia University, and there was a Tony Delaware, who had gone to San Francisco, living with other members of the group hoping to find a job.

It turned out that Leo Majors worked at the *St. Louis Post Dispatch* and was enrolled in some night classes at the University. "When I get enough money saved up," he told me, "I'm going to college full-time." But for now, it sounded like Leo was just barely making ends meet.

Johnny Dempsey was the only one who didn't seem to fit in with the rest of this crowd. Besides appearing much older, there was something else that made him less conforming, but I couldn't quite figure what it was. He smiled a lot and laughed with the others, but he was less talkative, and more cautious, and even though everyone included him in conversation, his input was always short and to the point.

I learned, though, as the evening went on, that Johnny was

a different kind of artist, and why he was accepted by this group where he seemed so out of place. Johnny had connections; he could obtain almost anything illegal or immoral, including morphine, cocaine, heroin, Benzedrine, marihuana hashish, or any other drug not readily available at the local pharmacy. If somebody wanted a gun, Johnny had a ready supplier for that too. I hoped there wasn't too much demand for firearms among this group.

"How long have you been a photographer?" Christopher asked me. He had temporarily broken away from his lengthy conversation with Andy.

"Not very long," I replied. "I'm still learning." That was better than telling the whole group that I had taken my first picture only a week ago.

"So, do you have pictures of your riverboat?"

"Oh, no. I didn't have a camera then."

"I wish I knew how to use a camera. Where I'm from in Colorado there are so many great things to photograph. We have the Rocky Mountains, you know..."

Christopher was a pleasant conversationalist, and I felt myself drawn toward his charming personality, just as Andy must have been. I had been noticing, too, that Marty was paying more attention to Christopher, as was Curtis who sat right next to him. When the two attractive young women appeared, and one of them sat in Christopher's lap—for the lack of any more available chairs—Marty and Curtis seemed a little put out and disappointed.

The other girl stood behind Leo, wrapped her arms around his neck and gave him a little kiss on the cheek. "How much longer are you gonna be here?" she asked Leo.

Leo glanced at his watch. "I don't know. Why?"

"Let's go over to the Liberty House. There's a good jazz band playing. Marcy and I feel like dancing."

The girls were certainly ready for dancing, in silky party

dresses with low-cut necklines, and multiple strings of color-ful beads and baubles dangling from around their necks.

Leo looked at me. "This is Sandy, my fiancé." Then he nodded toward the other girl who was heavily flirting with Cheechee. "And that's Sandy's friend, Marcy."

"How 'bout it, Sweetie?" Marcy enticed Christopher. It sounded more seductive than just a request to go dancing. He glanced over to Leo and winked. "If Leo and Sandy are going, then let's go."

Leo and Cheechee excused themselves, and then the four of them left.

Now that Leo was gone, I asked Frank, "Are they a couple, too?" I was referring to Christopher and Marcy.

Frank grinned a little, and then everyone but me and Andy expressed amusement with the question.

"No, not exactly," Frank said. "Cheechee plays around a lot, and it would surprise me if he ever settled down."

There was a lot yet to learn about Cheechee, but it was easy to determine that both women *and* men were attracted to Christopher Chapman's charisma. Cheechee had certainly added life to the party.

Johnny Dempsey got up from his chair. "Anyone needs any-thing," he said, "...you know where to find me." He made a quiet and unceremonious exit.

"Good night, Johnny," Marty said as Johnny walked by. "I'll catch up with you tomorrow." He reached for the beer pitch-er and poured what was left in the glasses of those who re-mained. Only one poker game was still in progress three ta-bles away. I could hear billiard balls clicking from some oth-er corner of the establishment, and there was still plenty of music and vocal activity spewing out from the barroom, but this party, for all practical purposes, was over. Andy and I had experienced our first encounter with the "Knights."

CHAPTER SIX

DURING the bus ride back to Sadie's house, Andy told me all that I had missed in his conversation with Christopher. "He was born poor," Andy began. "His father is a part-time janitor and a full-time alcoholic. Sounds like he stumbles around from one flophouse to another."

"What about his mother?" I asked.

"She tried to protect Chris and his brother from their dad, but she died when Chris was ten. So Chris didn't have any choice but to live with him."

"They lived in Colorado?"

"Yeah, Denver. Chris's brother was older and he'd left, and Chris said that by the time he was sixteen, he'd stolen no less than twenty cars."

"His brother stole twenty cars?"

"No. Chris did," Andy continued. "He dropped out of school, and then he got sent to a reformatory for a couple of years. And when he got out of there, he didn't have a home to go to, so he lived on the streets."

"So, how did he end up here?" I asked.

"He stole another car and drove it here to St. Louis."

"What an idiot!" I said.

"He's not an idiot," Andy corrected me in Christopher's defense. "When he was in the reform school they gave him IQ tests. He scored one-twenty."

With an IQ of 120, he was apparently as intelligent as he was charming, and I found it difficult to associate Cheechee as a car thief. He seemed much too refined for that. Obviously, he didn't have much going for him other than his astonishing good looks and an uninhibited personality, and he certainly knew how to play his charm for all it was worth.

"So, what does he do here? Steal cars? How does he make a living?"

"Says he hasn't stolen a single car since he's been here. He shares an apartment with Marty, and he actually has a job in a warehouse down on Walnut Street... oh... and he's writing a book."

Now it made sense to me why a car thief was admitted into the social clique we had just met. Marty had a rather tarnished background, too, and their personalities *did* seem compatible, and they both *did* have something in common with others in the group—they desired to be authors.

Andy had talked with Christopher at length and had gotten to know him better than I had. He liked Cheechee, and I was not going to disagree with him. Maybe Cheechee was trying to straighten himself out, but his recent past was still the makings of a juvenile delinquent.

I thought I should inform Andy of what I learned about Johnny Dempsey, the older man in the group. "Did you hear about Johnny?" I said.

"Well, Cheechee told me he gets Benzedrine from him, and they go to a tea pad together sometimes. He invited us to go with them sometime."

"And what did you say?"

"I told him maybe... we'd see."

"Kinda looks like we've been accepted into the group, eh?"

"Kinda looks that way," Andy replied. I sensed that he was just a little intrigued by it. And in a curious sort of way, so was I.

The next morning Sadie made us breakfast. "What did you do last night?" she asked while we ate our oatmeal. "It wasn't so very late when I heard you come in."

"Oh, we met some friends and had a few beers down-town," I said. At first I thought I had said too much, and now we would have to start answering all sorts of questions that we might not want to answer.

"Well, good for you," Sadie said. "You've made some new friends here. Did you have a good time?"

"Yes, ma'am," Andy said.

"Where did you meet these friends of yours?"

"In the theater district, on Grand Boulevard." I wasn't ex-actly lying; we did meet Marty there.

Sadie seemed impressed that we were frequenting the more intellectual sector of the city.

Then Andy reinforced the idea. "They're all writers, jour-nalists, musicians. They have a little get-together every week, and they invited us to join them."

"Musicians?" I said frowning. "Who else besides you in that group is a musician?"

"Curtis plays the saxophone, and Cheechee sings."

"Cheechee?" Sadie quizzed.

"His name is Christopher Chapman... first and last name begin with C-H... so they nicknamed him Cheechee."

Sadie wrinkled her brow in thought. "Well... I guess that makes perfect sense."

I knew then that Andy had learned a lot more good things about the members of the "Knights," while I learned about all the dark sides. But I was glad that Andy had steered the con-versation away from dope peddlers and car thieves.

"Sadie," I said. "Everybody in the group is an artist of some sort. Andy fits right in. So I have to get to be a good photographer. They might kick me out if I'm not *something*. So can you help me?"

"Well, sure," Sadie said. "We wouldn't want you to get kicked out of a club like that, now, would we?"

I smiled and frowned at the same time. I knew Sadie was able and willing to teach me more. I only hoped that I would have the right stuff in me to learn it.

It was Saturday and Sadie only had two appointments for portraits that morning. She was finished with them by 10:30. I had given Philip a bath, got him dressed and helped him with his breakfast, so Andy took him for a long walk and played with him while I received some more tutoring from Sadie. She taught me how to use flash bulbs when the natural light wasn't adequate, and how to make things appear differently by shooting the subject from different angles. "A fat man isn't so fat if he is facing the camera, but if his picture is made from his side profile... well, then he's fat."

She had me practice with several objects from around the house—a stack of pillows, Philip's stuffed blue rabbit, a potted plant from Sadie's porch, an ugly green pitcher from the kitchen cupboard—and when she developed the film later that afternoon, she could only give me praise. "It took me three months to learn what you've accomplished in a week," she told me. "Of course," she added, "I didn't have nearly as good a teacher," and then we both laughed.

But it was probably true. Much advancement in cameras and picture taking in general had occurred since Sadie learned the trade back in Philadelphia. She hadn't used a glass plate negative in nearly three years, and now she was eagerly looking forward to color photos, a process that was soon to be made practical. Sadie kept up with every new technique that came along. No, I couldn't have asked for a better teacher.

CHAPTER SEVEN

ANDY took the bus to St. Charles occasionally to visit his mom. He'd be gone for a few days, and sometimes I thought maybe he wouldn't come back to St. Louis. But he always did, and every Friday night we'd sit in the dim gas light at the Lion's Den drinking beer with the Knights. Andy's friendship with Cheechee grew stronger, and Cheechee even went with Andy to St. Charles a couple of times. I was glad that Andy was establishing new friendships—if anyone deserved to have friends, it was Andy. My relationship with the Knights elevated quickly, too, as I brought some of my "masterpiece" photographs for them to see.

By the end of November I had received my share of the insurance money for the loss of the Madison—$2,160.65—and I had discussed with Jesse on several occasions about combining our money to buy another boat, but Jesse was reluctant, said he'd rather work for Continental for a while before he made any decisions. It would be many months until Luke could obtain his pilot's license for barge tows, and that

41

seemed to be the most lucrative business on the river.

So as long as we had a place to live, and I could pitch in a little for groceries now and then, we decided to stay at Jesse's house and wait for the right opportunity, even after Sadie's regular babysitter got the cast off her leg. Andy didn't particularly want to move back to St. Charles; Mildred was staying with his mom, and even though he loved them both dearly, he thought living in a house with two "older" women would not be a good environment for him. I had to agree with his thinking, although I knew there were other reasons he wanted to stay in St. Louis. Cheechee was there, and his association with Curtis was getting him in line for an audition with a night club owner. But most of all, I think Andy was getting hooked on the new lifestyle he had tasted in the big city.

December brought chilly temperatures, but very little snow. It had been quite dry all over the Midwest for a couple of years, and farmers were plagued with drought conditions. Another year of the same would surely bring failure to many.

But there in St. Louis, we continued our association with the Knights; invitations to private parties started coming our way, and one night Johnny Dempsey and Cheechee took us to a tea pad in North St. Louis. Our first experience with marihuana was in a seedy neighborhood in a run-down brick building that should have been condemned. Cheechee said he knew some better places, and he'd take us to them sometime.

Expecting something a little more sophisticated, I might have been somewhat disappointed with some of the parties we attended at private homes in various parts of the city. When Marty invited us to a weekend soiree at George Sissel's place, I anticipated a dwelling of luxury to some degree. George wasn't a regular participant of the group, but he had showed up at the Lion's Den a few times. He had gone to law school a couple of years, but his life centered on parties and taverns more than on the fine points of the law. He had proven himself as the ultimate carouser, and his house parties were already legendary.

But instead of the deluxe *manor* that I expected, George's place was a deluxe *shack* with sagging porch and peeling paint. It was certainly large enough to accommodate a crowd, and despite its shabby appearance, there was certain splendor that had nothing to do with elegant rooms and plush furnishings. It was the people. This gathering could've been in a back alley and the atmosphere would be the same.

Andy and I had just arrived when Marty found us and led us to the kitchen where beer was being dispensed from a keg. We each got a glassful, and then Marty pushed our way through the mob into the parlor. Many of the people there we had seen and met before, but there were a few unfamiliar faces, too. A blue haze hung in the air, and since we had recently visited a tea pad, I recognized the hint of marihuana odor mingled with the cigarette smoke. Music wailed from the far side of the room, but it didn't come from a Victrola. I saw Curtis with his saxophone but I couldn't see who was *trying* to play the piano; whoever it was could have used a few lessons from Beth Lorado. When Curtis spotted us, he abruptly ended the tune and called out to Andy. Without any hesitation, Andy threaded his way across the room, and by the time he reached the piano, Curtis had leaned close to the piano player's ear and whispered something. There was an immediate vacancy on the piano bench.

It wasn't surprising that Andy was so willing to play; he hadn't entertained a crowd since the Madison burned. I could tell that he seemed eager, and when he started hammering out the tune that had sort of become his theme song—*Happy Days Are Here Again*—the crowd began cheering and dancing, as if they had been waiting for the main attraction. I thought back about the time when "Andrew" first took to the piano on our riverboat, nervous and uneasy, playing that very same song for a highly sophisticated audience. They had loved him and his music, as had every group of excursionists since.

It was no different here. The mood of the crowd seemed to change, and there could be little doubt that Andy was suddenly in control. He picked the songs, and Curtis followed his lead. I couldn't help but think that Curtis was as good on the saxophone as Andy on the piano. They made a good team. It didn't take long for Cheechee to appear at the piano, and as if it had been rehearsed, he started vocalizing and soon led a sing-along with a large number of partiers gathered around.

Another mood changed, too. I was chatting with Marty while Andy and Curtis were getting really warmed up, and he seemed to enjoy their sounds as much as anyone did. But when Cheechee became part of the act, Marty stiffened and sneered toward the musicians. Whatever problem there was, it must have had something to do with Cheechee. I knew he and Marty shared an apartment; Cheechee had been avoiding any close encounters with Marty for some time; there must have been some sort of conflict.

"What's wrong?" I asked Marty.

"Oh, nothing," he said, but he looked at me as if to say *mind your own business,* and so I didn't ask any more questions.

A long while later Andy, Curtis and Cheechee must have decided to end the show, or else they were just taking a break. When I realized the music was absent from all the other noise, I noticed only Curtis coming out of the kitchen with a tall glass of beer.

"You and Andy sound real good together," I complimented him.

"Thanks," Curtis replied. "It's fun to play with a *good* piano player for a change... and Andy is *really good.*"

"Yeah, I know. I hear you're setting up an audition for

him."

"Actually, he just *had* his audition."

"He did? But I thought—"

"I told Harry we'd be playing here tonight and that he should stop by to hear Andy play."

"Who's Harry?"

"He books acts for the theaters and night clubs."

"Why here?"

"So Andy wouldn't be nervous. He told me he might be a little jittery in a place like the *Empress* or the *Arcadia*, especially for a formal audition. He didn't even know Harry was here watching and listening."

"So, how do you think it went?"

"Harry liked him. He gave me a wink and thumbs up just before he left."

"Does Andy know?"

"Not yet. I haven't talked to him."

"So... what will Harry do for Andy?"

Curtis put his hand on my shoulder, a serious expression on his face. "Whatever you do, don't tell Andy that this could turn into something big. It prob'ly won't. Harry just looks for people like Andy and me to fill in on off nights for maybe an hour... maybe just fifteen minutes. But I usually make enough to pay the rent and buy groceries."

"Well... you get paid to play music. Then you're a professional musician."

"I don't consider myself a professional... yet. But I wanna be someday, and this is a good way to get started. Actually, Andy is more professional than I am. He had a full-time job as an entertainer... on your riverboat, didn't he?"

"Well, yeah, sort of... but he did other things, too."

"Yeah, I know... he told me he was just a cabin boy. But I know the real reason he was there... to be the entertainment."

"Sure. I guess you're right, Curtis." I looked around. "Where *is* Andy? Did you see where he went?"

"He and Cheechee went off somewhere."

"You mean... they left?"

"No. They're prob'ly upstairs... said they had something important to talk about."

By the time Andy and Cheechee showed up again, the party had progressed from the earlier joyous feel to drunken disorder. Too many people had consumed too much alcohol; temperaments began to clash as voices raised and punches were thrown. Then the fighting seemed contagious, and when blood started to spill, Curtis suggested that we should leave.

"Let's get outa here," he said. "My car is just around the corner." He dodged a couple of swinging fists getting to the piano to grab his saxophone case, and then Andy, Cheechee and I followed him out the front door and down the sidewalk to the end of the block. Andy and Cheechee piled into the rear seat of the old Ford sedan, and I sat in the front with Curtis. That car was like an oasis, a safe haven from the brawl that had developed in George's house. I was so thankful to escape that I barely noticed the freezing cold night.

CHAPTER EIGHT

IT had been nearly 2 a.m. when Curtis dropped off me and Andy at Jesse's house. An exciting night had us both exhausted; we went right to bed without hardly talking. I think I was asleep before my head hit the pillow, and I think Andy was sleeping by the time we reached the top of the stairs.

I sensed the bright sunshine without opening my eyes. The night had seemed to pass by so quickly. Philip was patting my chest. "Unca Will! Doo! Wake up! Time for brefus!" He had climbed up on the bed and sat between me and Andy.

"Okay, okay," Andy grumbled. "We're getting up."

I squinted at the clock on the nightstand. It was almost 9:00. I couldn't remember when I had slept that late. Philip bounced on the mattress a few times, then jumped to the floor and scurried out of the room babbling something that I couldn't understand. His footfalls on the steps were quite distinct, and then I heard Sadie downstairs. "Did you wake up those two sleepy heads?" "Yeah!" Philip giggled. "Good boy," Sadie said. "Their breakfast will get cold." And then their voices trailed away into the kitchen.

I could smell pancakes and fresh coffee.

Sadie had become less inquisitive about our nighttime activities; she knew we were usually at the Lion's Den with the Knights on Friday evenings, and carousing on Saturdays.

Maybe she didn't want to make any fuss about it, or perhaps she was respecting our privacy, or maybe she just didn't care.

"Have you heard from Jesse?" I asked at the breakfast table.

Philip looked sad and shook his little head. "Daddy's not coming home today."

"Yes, as a matter of fact," Sadie replied. "I heard from him day before yesterday... they're in Baton Rouge."

"Coming this way?" I asked.

"No... they're headed back to New Orleans... maybe two weeks until they're back here again. But at least he'll make it home for Christmas."

It seemed strange not to be around Jesse all the time like it had been when we still had the boat. Those years had given me the best sense of security in my entire life. But perhaps this was a good challenge for me, too; to not rely on Big Brother all the time; to experience independence; to see what else life had to offer away from the river. I had to admit that I had overcome my fear of venturing alone too far from the Madison. I had overcome my hatred for the big city. I had made a lot of new friends. I had learned photography, and I was eager to master it.

This had been a good experience for Andy, too. He had finally severed his mother's apron strings that kept him somewhat restricted. He seemed content with his new lifestyle and comfortable with his new friends. Until now, Andy had been a bit shy, but spending so much time with Cheechee and his uninhibited personality had opened a release valve, and now the real Andy was pouring out like an overturned syrup bottle. Whether he knew it or not, last night might have been a new beginning.

"Andy had an audition last night," I blurted out. I couldn't help myself.

"I did not," Andy said.

"Did so," I retaliated. "Curtis told me all about it when you and Cheechee went off somewhere."

"What are you talking about? I didn't have an audition last night."

"Sure you did. Harry was there at the party. He heard you play... and he liked you."

"Harry was there? How do you know that?"

"Curtis told me... he had Harry come because you'd be nervous for an audition at one of the big night clubs, and you'd play better if you didn't know he was there." I turned to Sadie. "You should've seen it, Sadie. Andy at the piano, Curtis on the saxophone, and Cheechee sang. They had that house jumpin'!" I bobbed my head and waved my arms as I spoke for a little more effect.

Philip laughed loudly and banged his spoon on the table.

"Doesn't surprise me," Sadie said. "I've heard Andy play."

"Yeah. When he started playin' his theme song, it was like everybody in the place recognized it and they all started cheerin' and dancin'."

Sadie eyed Andy. "You know, don't you, that you stole that song from *President Franklin D. Roosevelt?*"

Andy beamed a smile wider than Grand Boulevard. "Yeah, but I don't think he'll mind." Then he turned to me. "What else did Curtis tell you?"

"Just that you'd be filling in sometimes... with Curtis, I think... but I wasn't supposed to tell you any of this."

"Will!" Sadie scolded.

"I couldn't help it," I pleaded. "Andy deserves to know about it." Then I looked Andy square in the eyes. "And don't you tell Curtis that you heard it from me."

"Okay..." Andy laughed. "I won't tell him... blabber mouth."

"Well, congratulations, Andy!" Sadie said. "Even if Will *wasn't* supposed to tell you... I'm glad for you."

"Better not congratulate me yet," Andy said. "I haven't played a single note anywhere, yet."

"No, but you will," Sadie assured him.

"And I'll be there to take your picture!" I added.

Andy seemed quite pleased, but I sensed that something was troubling him, too. After we finished breakfast, he said to me: "Will, let's go in the parlor and play our song." And then in a low whisper he added, "We gotta talk."

"If it's about the audition last night—"

"No... something else."

Whatever Andy wanted to talk about, he was guarding it from Sadie. He pushed me into the parlor, we sat on the piano bench, and as usual, I started playing *Down by the Riverside* with my one-finger style. He joined in with *April in Paris*. While we played, he said in a low voice, "We should move out of here."

"Why?" I said.

"We're probably a bother to Sadie."

"No we're not. Sadie doesn't mind us being here." There was some other reason for Andy's suggestion. I stopped playing and stared at him, waiting for further explanation.

"Cheechee is having some problems," Andy continued. He saw that I wasn't buying the bother-to-Sadie reason. "He's found a place to move to, and he wants *us* to move in with him."

"What kind of trouble is he in? Steal another car?"

"No, he's not in *any trouble*," Andy corrected me. "He has *problems*."

"Okay... so what kind of problems?"

"Cheechee is staying with Johnny Dempsey now... for the time being. It was the one place he knew he could go without an invitation. And actually, I think he stayed at Curtis's place last night."

"I thought he was sharing an apartment with Marty."

"He is... or maybe I should say he *was.*"

"What happened?"

"Marty wanted Cheechee to get him a car, and Cheechee said no, he didn't want to do that anymore."

"So that's why Marty was acting a little strange last night."

"Well, that's not all. When Cheechee wouldn't get him a car, Marty demanded some other favors if he wanted to keep staying in Marty's apartment."

"What... oh... you mean..."

"Yeah, and when Cheechee refused, things started getting ugly. That's when he packed his bags and went to Johnny's."

"So... why doesn't he just stay at Johnny's place?"

"Well, that's the problem. He's having almost the same thing happening there, too."

"Johnny wants him to steal cars?"

"No."

I went back to playing *Down by the Riverside* again; Andy played the usual backup. It gave me some time to think. All this information was piling up too quickly.

"Okay," I finally said. "Marty's dirty looks weren't intended for Cheechee last night... they were intended for *you*, 'cause you and Cheechee have been spending a lot of time together lately."

Andy nodded. "That's probably right."

"You and Cheechee..."

Andy's face turned a mild red. "We're friends, Will."

"Well, I thought he and Marty were friends; and Johnny, too."

"They are."

"Then, why you?"

"I guess I'm different."

"How?"

"I didn't stumble and trip over my own feet running to him, or drool all over him. That happens to him a lot. He's a pretty handsome guy, in case you haven't noticed."

I had noticed. The very first time we met at the Lion's Den.

"Cheechee is trying really hard to straighten out his life," Andy went on. There was certain compassion in his voice. "He's really a good person... not like some of the others."

"But he drinks and he smokes dope."

"Will. Listen to yourself. So have we. I s'pose that's water you drink at the Lion's Den every Friday night, and how many tea pads have we been to lately?"

"A few. But I haven't stolen twenty cars or been in jail."

"That's all behind him, now. Will, you've told me about *your* life in Milwaukee. You jumped a freight train and ran away when you were fourteen. You stole shirts and jeans from backyard clotheslines and you raided gardens and porches for food. How do you think your life would've turned out if you hadn't met up with Jesse?"

Andy made a solid point. It was true. I could have easily turned into a hardened criminal if Jesse hadn't taken me in and steered me away from my life of petty theft. I hadn't thought about it for a long time, but I used to think about it a lot. Now, Andy was showing me, once again, how important Jesse's companionship and brotherly love had always been to me, and I could clearly understand what he was trying to do for Cheechee. I think I was beginning to soften.

"The place Cheechee found is just four or five blocks from Grand Boulevard, fully furnished, ready to move in. You can have your own room if you want. And Will, there's a piano! Twenty-five bucks a month. We can split it three ways. I know you can afford it, Will. You've got more money than most banks. I've got some money saved, and it sounds like I'll be working again soon. Cheechee makes enough to pay his share, too, so how 'bout it? What d'ya think? We can go see the place tomorrow."

"You see it yet? I hope it's not a shack like George's place."

"No, I haven't seen it yet, but Cheechee says it's real nice."

There was no doubt in my mind; Andy was sincere, and from that first time we met face to face in the woods and I touched him to make sure he was real I had always known that his heart was in the right place. Now he was trying to be convincing, and it was working quite well.

"You really like Cheechee, don't you?"

"Yes. He's a good person inside, and he deserves my— *our*—friendship."

CHAPTER NINE

THANKS to Curtis and his old car, the move to our new place went quite smoothly. I was afraid that Sadie and Jesse would pressure me and Andy with some opposition to our moving into our own house, but they were actually quite supportive. We would have waited until after the holidays, but Cheechee's situation was more urgent, and Andy and I were feeling awful about him being all alone with no place to go on Christmas.

Good old Jesse, the thoughtful and caring soul that he is, didn't hesitate to invite us all to their house for Christmas Eve supper. When we arrived, another pleasant surprise awaited us: Andy's mom and dad, Beth and Marion Lorado were there, too, and shortly after we arrived, Luke and Reggie showed up. I hadn't seen them since the Madison fire, although Andy said he had bumped into Reggie one day somewhere in town. So that Christmas turned into a grand reunion. Mildred would have been there, but she had gone to visit her sister in Kansas City for the holidays.

Cheechee was the only "stranger" in the entire group. Beth Lorado had met him when he went to St. Charles with Andy, but he was a new face to everyone else. Of course, his charming personality had no difficulty to quickly develop nothing less than stellar relationships with everyone there, including Marion Lorado, who usually warmed up to anyone slower than grass grows. Perhaps Beth had prompted him to be civil to Andy's new friend, but it seemed that Marion's acceptance of Cheechee was sincere. Either Cheechee did possess some magical power, or I had witnessed an amazing change in the man who had once considered me and Jesse "river trash."

Although I didn't consider any of our riverboat family high-class snobs, we had become a more sophisticated lot while catering to the upper class patrons who traveled on the Madison. Naturally, I was concerned about the questions that might be asked of Cheechee. His background was a little stained, and I knew for sure that the purification process was not yet absolute. Christopher Chapman was still the makings of a juvenile delinquent.

"Where are you originally from?" Jesse asked Cheechee.

"I was born and grew up in Denver, Colorado."

"Your family is still there?"

"My mother passed away when I was ten years old. My older brother moved on to bigger and better things, and my father suffered from mental and physical depression, and he has been institutionalized."

"Oh," Jesse replied. "Sorry to hear that."

"There was little I could do to help the situation. The state looked after me until I was old enough to be on my own, and when I realized that I couldn't be of any help to my father, I scraped together my resources and came to St. Louis."

Oh boy! Cheechee could charm! But that's what I liked about him. He carried himself with such confidence, and he could express himself so eloquently, and he did it all in such admirably pleasant style. I kept thinking all the while he chatted with Jesse: *How could've this prince of a guy stolen even* one *car?*

Sadie and Beth had been working nearly all day preparing

a magnificent feast—roast turkey and all the trimmings. The wonderful aroma that filled the entire house was nearly indescribable, and all the food tasted even better. Perhaps, by force of habit, when the meal was finished Andy and I dug into the clean-up chores, helping Sadie and Beth with clearing the table and washing dishes. When the kitchen and dining room were in riverboat spotless condition, we all joined the others in the parlor around a festive Christmas tree. Little Philip was so excited. He was old enough now to remember past Christmases, and he had a pretty good idea of what to expect.

Everyone received gifts; even Cheechee got a stocking cap and mittens that Beth had knitted, just like she had given me the winter that I stayed at the Lorado home. This year, she and Marion gave both me and Andy gentleman's walking sticks—something we had noticed and commented about many times when we saw the wealthy men aboard the Madison using them. They remembered.

Andy and I had gifts for everyone, too. We had been thinking ahead in October when we got the *St. Louis Cardinals—1934 World Series Champions* baseball caps for Reggie and Luke. They were both Chicago Cubs fans, but they liked the caps anyway. Philip loved his big yellow teddy bear that he immediately named *"Cuddles."*

I would cherish my gift from Sadie and Jesse for years. When I opened it, I think my heart nearly stopped; I was totally speechless as I held the 35mm *Leica* camera and stared at Sadie with my lower jaw hanging like a porch swing.

"It's just like mine," Sadie said. "It's the newest model. Do you like it?"

"I... I..." I still couldn't say anything. Words just wouldn't come out of my mouth. I jumped up and bounded to where Sadie and Jesse sat together on the couch. I threw my arms around them both and squeezed out the most sincere hug of my life. When I finally gained my composure again, all I could say was "Thank you." I felt rather foolish for not saying more, but the look in their eyes told me I didn't need to say anything more.

I remained in awe for quite some time as I closely examined the *Leica*. Sadie had included six rolls of film and two dozen flash bulbs. By the time I loaded some film, Philip was yawning and ready for bed; he and Cuddles were my first subject with my brand new *Leica*.

We had already finished off a couple of bottles of excellent local wine that Marion brought from a St. Charles winery when Jesse carried in from the back porch a case of imported ale. He'd purchased it in New Orleans. Andy serenaded us for a while, and Cheechee even sang three or four songs and as usual, no one would let the evening end without hearing Andy and I play our *Down by the Riverside/April in Paris* duet. It was certainly a joyous night.

I had plenty of time to reflect on the past as I shot a few more pictures of everyone enjoying the Christmas holiday. In my entire lifetime, I would never be able to repay Jesse for all he had done for me; I still admired Luke and Reggie for putting up with me and being my friends.

As I listened to Andy play, I watched Marion Lorado and Cheechee converse as if they had known each other for years. I thought about that Christmas Eve when Marion finally took notice of Andrew's talent and accepted him for who he is.

I smiled inside.

CHAPTER TEN

THE house on Prairie Avenue was a modest, two-story affair, nicely furnished with the basic needs—nothing fancy or extravagant, but adequate.

Andy and I were accustomed to housekeeping—skills we learned aboard the riverboat. As cabin boys we had been involved with everything from galley work and serving meals for sixty or seventy people, to sweeping floors and putting clean sheets on beds. Of course, in this house there were fewer people to clean up after—just us—so it was a lot less work.

But Cheechee, on the other hand, was not accustomed to such chores, and he required a little "training" to conform to our standards. Anything he might have learned from his mother was so long ago that he'd forgotten it all. And living with an incompetent, drunken father certainly taught him nothing but bad habits, which soon surfaced. But Cheechee was such a pleasant person to be with, polite and considerate of others. Andy and I tolerated his shortcomings until we got him "trained." Perhaps we were a little hard on him at times; we had just come from an environment on the excursion boat where tidiness was mandatory, and our good habits followed us here.

He didn't know how to cook, so whenever the opportunity presented itself, we conducted cooking class. Within a few weeks he was doing his fair share of the meal preparation, and he even seemed to enjoy it. Naturally, his entrées sometimes weren't what we would expect from the Madison's chef, but at least it was edible, and he *was* trying, and he *was* getting better with practice.

Cheechee went off to work every morning, Monday to Friday. He walked half a block to the bus stop where he boarded a *St. Louis Public Service Company* bus, and he said he had to change buses only once to get to the warehouse where he worked on Walnut Street. I had expected that he would be out late partying almost every night, and I feared that he would be influencing me and Andy to do the same. But I was surprised to see Cheechee at home most of the time. Every night he sat diligently at a writing desk, or sometimes at the kitchen table, or sometimes in his room, with pencil and notebook. He was working on something he called *"If I Could Steal the Stars."* He kept telling us that he would let us read it when he had more of it written. But for now he said it was a story about a young man and his destiny. I was never one to pry into another person's private affairs if I hadn't been invited. It was clearly obvious that Cheechee wasn't ready to share the story just yet, so I certainly wasn't about to invade his privacy. I remained curious, though, and I continued to let him know that I was still interested.

"Will," he told me. "Believe me, I will want you and Andy

J.L. Fredrick

to be the first to see it... when it's ready."

Curtis Owens was the only one of the Knights who knew exactly where we lived, and in no uncertain terms we made it clear that we wanted to keep it that way. He kind of understood the problems Cheechee had with Marty and Johnny, but Cheechee hadn't been quite as explicit with Curtis as he had been with Andy and me. Even though we still considered them our friends, and they didn't ever pose any difficulties at the Friday night gatherings at the Lion's Den, we didn't need them stalking our house waiting for the first opportunity to confront Cheechee alone. But we trusted Curtis—we had to—he had helped us move to our new place, and he came over to practice with Andy a couple times a week. I think, too, that he was beginning to enjoy the solitude, the privacy, the safety that our place offered. His place, not much more than a single room with a closet, a hot plate, and a shared bathroom on the second floor over a hardware store, didn't provide much in the line of hominess or cozy comfort. Andy and I had been there a couple of times, and although we had grown to like Curtis, we had little desire to return to his bachelor pad for frequently repeated visits. I could easily understand why he took pleasure in our place so much.

About the middle of January, Curtis appeared at our door one night. He seemed all keyed up about something, and I was sure it wasn't "Bennies" or marihuana that had him bouncing off the walls.

"Where's Andy?" he asked. He almost ran me over getting into the parlor. "Hi, Cheechee!" he sang out when he saw Cheechee sitting at the writing desk. "ANDY! WHERE ARE YOU?" he called out. His excitement caught us all off-guard.

Andy came trotting down the stairs. "Curtis! What's goin' on?"

Curtis had good reason to be excited. "You and me are in

60

the line-up at the *Arcadia* three nights next week! Half-hour pre-show for Benny Goodman!"

Andy's jaw dropped and he stopped dead in his tracks on the bottom step.

"Harry just told me tonight... said we're a perfect opener."

Andy still stood there speechless.

Cheechee rushed over and put an arm around each of them. "Congratulations, you two! This is great!" Then he threw both arms around Andy, engulfing him in an enthusiastic hug. "I'm so happy for you, Andy. This is what you've been waiting for."

I had to get in on the hugging and handshaking, too. I was truly happy for both of them.

"It's a sell-out crowd," Curtis continued. "Harry's gettin' us a hundred and fifty bucks for the three nights... that's seventy-five each. Not bad for three nights."

Now I was really happy for Andy. That was more money than he had made on the Madison. Of course, his tip jar always filled there every night, too, and I didn't know how much that amounted to, but this sounded pretty darn good!

Andy and Curtis practiced at least two hours every afternoon at our house for the rest of the week. I was usually at Sadie's studio learning and helping her as much as I could. By then Sadie had taught me how to develop film and how to operate the apparatus that enlarges and transfers the image onto paper. So there were always plenty of things for me to do, and it helped sharpen my abilities. I was well on my way towards a new career, and all because Philip's babysitter broke her leg.

CHAPTER ELEVEN

WE didn't have to ride a bus or street car to the Lion's Den Friday night; Curtis was already at our house for the afternoon practice with Andy. We all went together in his car. Friday night at the Lion's Den wasn't a lot different than any other Friday night had been there, except for a couple of new faces that Andy or I didn't recognize. Everyone else seemed to know them, though. Milo Lipinski had just returned from New York, and Tony Delaware had been on the west coast. Because both had been away for several months, they were receiving a good share of the attention. Milo was here for just a short visit during a semester break at Columbia University, but Tony seemed unsure about his next move. He had worked for a short time in California; it didn't last.

After the initial chatter among just about everyone over where Milo and Tony had been and what they had been doing, Milo and Marty settled into a conversation about poetry; Milo had given Marty a copy of *The Vision* by William Butler Yeats, and they were discussing its contents, Milo convinced that "this is what poetry should be." I had never heard of Yeats, so I had no idea what they were talking about.

Tony and Cheechee talked about Denver; apparently Tony had stopped there for a while on his way back from San Francisco.

Frank and Johnny were talking about some parties they had recently attended, and I told Leo about my new camera; he was interested in my progress with photography.

Curtis and Andy were just waiting for the right moment to announce their first gig together on stage. It would be a big night for them; certainly they would want everyone to know. But Curtis's declaration came with little fanfare. "Andy and I won't be here next Friday night. We'll be performing."

It only took a few seconds for that to sink in. "Who's having a party?" Milo asked.

"It's not a party," Curtis returned. "We're playing at the *Arcadia* Thursday, Friday and Saturday."

"Yeah, right," Marty said sarcastically. "I saw in the newspaper that Benny Goodman is playing there next weekend."

"He is," Curtis replied. "We're the opener."

"You... are gonna be the warm-up for Benny Goodman?"

Everyone at the table had taken notice of the banter, and all eyes shifted to Curtis as he just nodded and smiled. Andy was grinning, too, and in the few moments of silence while everyone digested the news, he looked around to each face, as if expecting reactions other than dropped jaws and silence.

Nearly everyone had heard Andy and Curtis making music at George's party, so they were very much aware of the talent and showmanship they commanded. There was no question that they were both capable. That an opportunity like this should come to members of our little group was the real surprise. Local radio stations were airing the new Benny Goodman "swing" music, and even though it was 11:30 at night, the syndicated radio program *"Let's Dance"* with Goodman and his band as one of the regular performers had become quite popular in St. Louis. People were excited about the new kind of music and they were eager to see and hear the clarinet-playing band leader, Benny Goodman in person.

Then the reactions came. "That's great!" "Wonderful!" "Fantastic!" "Can we still get tickets?"

"From what I've been told," Curtis said, "It's standing room only."

"Well... that's okay. I'll be there!" "Me too." "We'll all be there, for sure."

After all the congratulatory remarks were delivered there was a new wave of chatter going around the table about which night to go to the *Arcadia Ballroom*, who was going with who, and transportation arrangements. It seemed that everyone favored Friday night; the Lion's Den would be without the Knights of the Square Table the next week.

Milo seemed a bit standoffish to me, and even though he had said that he would go to the *Arcadia* next Friday night, his sole focus otherwise was Marty and poetry. He and Marty did have New York in common, so I guess they had plenty to talk about.

But I liked Tony Delaware. Much like Cheechee, he was attracting attention from more than one person there. He had apparently been quite popular before he left for California, and it wasn't difficult to tell why. Good-humored and talkative, his smile must've been permanently molded on his face; I didn't see him without it all evening. His teeth weren't perfectly straight and his hair looked like he'd just climbed out of bed, but it was those things that helped make him the unique character that he was.

CHAPTER TWELVE

JUST a block off Grand Boulevard on Olive, the *Arcadia* packed in a crowd—even for a Thursday night. Young and old alike were there to see the band they had been hearing on the radio. The "King of Swing" was there in flesh and blood, and no one thought the seventy-five cents admission was too much to pay to have Benny Goodman set their feet to dancing. Spirits were high, and it promised to be an enjoyable evening. I was excited for Andy and Curtis; that afternoon while they were getting ready (Curtis was spending most of his time at our house now) I could sense their energized emotion, although they were trying very hard to conceal it. Harry had outfitted them with tuxedos from a theater's stage ward-robe. Curtis wore black, and Andy wore white, and I have to admit they looked quite stunning. But they chose to carry their tuxes with them on the ride to the ball-room where they would change in a back-stage dressing room that they had been assigned.

Armed with my new *Leica* 35mm camera, I parted with Curtis and Andy in the parking lot; they headed for a side entrance that led to the back-stage dressing rooms, while Cheechee and I made our way toward the front entrance where I was supposed to meet Leo. He had arranged for me to hook up with a reporter/photographer from the *Post Dispatch,* the newspaper where Leo worked. Not only would I get some front-and-center pictures of Andy and Curtis—*and Benny Goodman*—but perhaps I would learn a few pointers, too.

Keith Blake was tall and slender, thirtyish, high cheek bones and square chin that were covered with a day's growth of black stubble. His pinstriped suit was far from being fresh, like he'd been in it all day. A narrow brimmed hat sat cocked back on his closely-cropped black head of hair.

Leo introduced us. "Keith Blake... this is Will Madison." He had already filled in Mr. Blake about who I was and why I was there. Cheechee was already headed for the entrance in the line for people who didn't yet have a ticket.

"You're the riverboat guy," Blake said as he shook my hand.

"Yes, sir, Mr. Blake, I am... but how—?"

"I'm a newspaper reporter. It's my job to remember stuff like that. I took pictures of your burning boat... and please call me *Blake.*"

I thought back to that night and recalled the many reporters and photographers lined up on the levee, flashbulbs exploding every three or four seconds. With all the smoke and the flashes and the chaos, it might have been a war zone.

"So it was *your* pictures of the fire that I saw in the newspaper?"

"If you saw the front page of the *Post* the next day... yeah, you saw my pictures." He eyed me suspiciously. "You're kind of young to own a riverboat."

"Actually, I was just a junior partner with my older brother, Jesse Madison."

Blake squinted a little. "Oh, yeah, now I remember... there were three of you."

"Yeah. The third partner was Luke Jackson. He and Jesse are on a barge towboat now."

Blake stared for a moment at my camera suspended on a strap around my neck. *"Leica,"* he said. "That's a fine camera." Then he held his up where I could see it better. Same camera.

"Okay," Blake said as he peered over the people scrambling to get into the Arcadia. "You got a ticket?" he asked.

"No, not yet," I replied.

"That's good. You don't need one. If you had one, you could give it to your friend. Just let me do the talking when we get to the ticket taker inside."

"I'll see ya later," I told Leo, and then we pushed toward the entrance.

"Hi Blake," the ticket collector said.

"Hi, Tommy. This is Will Madison," Blake said as he laid a hand on my shoulder. "He's with me... a new trainee... and if you ever see him here alone, you treat him just like you'd treat me... got it?"

Tommy gave me a thorough inspection, as if memorizing every detail of my image. "Glad to meet you, Will," he said as he briefly shook my hand. "Enjoy the show, and I hope you get some good pictures. Blake will show you where to go."

Apparently, Blake was on first name basis with the ticket taker, and his position with the newspaper obviously gave him an inside edge at the *Arcadia*—perhaps any theater in the whole city where well-known performers attracted reporters and photographers.

Blake led me through the inner doors into the ballroom and then down along an outer wall behind a large seating area toward the right end of the stage. From there we went directly to stage center, only ten feet back from the footlights. Several other photographers were seated on folding chairs there, too, in a reserved little area just for them.

"You'll never need to pay your way in here, Will," Blake whispered to me. "...As long as you have that dandy camera hangin' 'round your neck."

The next ten minutes seemed like hours. I could hear scuffing noises and muffled voices from behind the stage curtain, obviously some last-minute preparations. Then the house lights dimmed and a big, bright, round circle of light projected against the curtain from a balcony. A distinguished-looking, silver-haired man in a black tuxedo and top hat stepped into the spotlight in front of a microphone. "Ladies and gentlemen," he began, as if he were announcing the opening act at a three-ring circus. "With great pleasure," he continued, "the Arcadia proudly presents to you... the King of Swing himself, Benny Goodman."

The crowd hushed from its anxious rumbling, mingling voices.

"But first, please welcome and enjoy Saint Louis's newest jazz duo... The Gaslight Knights!"

I was taken by complete surprise as the spotlight faded to nothing and the curtain rose. I had expected to see Andy and Curtis open the show. But then I heard the familiar sounds of Andy's theme song, *Happy Days Are Here Again*, and then a blue-tinted spotlight beam splashed on the stage, exposing a brilliantly shining baby grand piano, white tuxedo, and Andy's big grin. Just as I had heard them practice at the house, Curtis joined in with his saxophone, and another blue spotlight found its mark on him. In this great hall, with the help of amplifiers, they sounded fantastic!

A few seconds went by and the crowd was still silent, waiting patiently to decide on cheering or booing of this new duo, "The Gaslight Knights." I held my breath in anticipation, and then I felt the joy of relief as the hoots and cheers and whistles and claps rose to a brief roar, and then descended to a rhythmic clapping and shuffling of dancing shoes.

Blake leaned toward me and spoke in my ear: "Aren't you going to record this first moment? It's the important one, you know. Never comes again."

I was so excited for Andy and Curtis and so wrapped up in the reactions from the audience that I had nearly forgotten why I wanted to be so close to the stage. I was so glad that Sadie had coached me on taking pictures in this type of light. I got my camera set, focused, and clicked off several shots.

They played six more lively numbers in their allotted time, and when they ended, Andy and Curtis joined together at center stage, bowing and waving to a pumped-up, cheering crowd. All I remember of Benny Goodman saying when he was introduced was, "Good evening ladies and gentlemen... what an act to follow!"

CHAPTER THIRTEEN

HARRY, the booking agent, had been so impressed by the performance and the crowd's reaction to Andy and Curtis that he lined them up with more appearances right away. It seemed that every week he was calling on them with another date at another night club, hotel, or dance hall. Cheechee and I tagged along a few times, but eventually, the thrill lessened for us. We resumed our regular routine on Friday nights at the Lion's Den, and sometimes, depending on what time Andy and Curtis performed, they would show up a little later, too.

Now that Curtis and Andy were established in the entertainment scene, Cheechee and I had more time together. Not that our relationship with Andy ever diminished—if anything, it became stronger. But Andy needed his time for arranging and practicing new music with Curtis. Both of them took performing quite seriously, and why shouldn't they? They were making good money. Not all the engagements paid as well as that first one opening for Benny Goodman, but they were still fairing quite well.

In spite of our differences in character, I couldn't help but feel a strange closeness to Cheechee; he reminded me, somehow, of a long-lost brother. It wasn't the same kind of feelings I had toward Big Brother Jesse—there could be nothing that would ever compare to that. Perhaps it was just Cheechee's magical, mysterious charm that drew me in, or maybe it was because I could relate so well to his broken family history that was so similar to my own. Whatever it was, I found my admiration for him growing, and as the weeks passed, I sensed that he began to consider me an important part of his life, too.

He'd come home from his workday about the same time in the afternoon that I would arrive after working a few hours at Sadie's studio. Cheechee's dirty work clothes clung to his muscular form so gracefully, as if you couldn't buy a better fit from a custom tailor.

Andy and Curtis would either be deeply involved with a practice session, or they would be away searching the music stores for sheet music, or off for the evening playing a gig somewhere. So supper, much of the time, was just the two of us, and quite frequently a hamburger at the *Dixie Sandwich Shop* seemed more appealing than cooking. We'd hop on a bus down to Olive Street, and then catch a streetcar toward the river to Sixth and Pine. There were probably closer places to get a hamburger, but we favored the *Dixie*. Many hours were spent there eating and talking, learning about each other, and swapping information about all our mutual friends.

It seemed that all my current acquaintances were intellectuals, or, they were casting a shadow on that very fine line, on the other side of which lurked slinking criminals. Regardless of his tainted past, Cheechee's intelligence was genuine and impressive for someone who had spent a good share of his early life on skid row with an alcoholic father among vagrants and bums, and another good share in jail, leaving little time for education. But his criminal side was not that of a sneering and threatening type; he'd made some foolish mistakes, and his youthful inexperience had gotten him caught a time or two. Now he was simply a kid tremendously excited with life. He was a wild outburst of American joy that blew in on the West wind, seeking something new. In Denver, he'd spent a lot of time in the public library—when he wasn't in jail. He'd carry stacks of books to the pool hall or climb fire escapes of abandoned buildings to the attics where he spent days reading and hiding from the law. Here, now, he was applying his knowledge, trying to make a better life.

"I really don't regret all that I've done in the past," Cheechee told me. "It's true... I did steal a bunch of cars back in Denver, but only for joy rides, never for financial gains. The rightful owners got their cars back. And yeah, I did some jail time, and a couple of years in reform school. No, I didn't have much of a home life. But it's all helped me learn about the real world, and all that reading helped me understand who I am."

I had listened to all this sort of information trickle into our conversations over a period of time; there was ever-present consistency and the "facts" didn't ever change, so it didn't appear that he was inventing the stories as he went along. It seemed like he was feeding me a lot of guarded details about his life that he had not shared with the rest of the Knights of the Square Table—with Andy, perhaps, but not the others— and I began to associate his verbal offerings with his secretive writing. "So the book you're writing... it's about you, ain't it?"

Cheechee took a bite of his hamburger, smiling while he chewed. "I'll let you read some of it soon, Will... I promise."

CHAPTER FOURTEEN

ONE rainy March Saturday evening Cheechee and I had just settled into a corner table by the window at the *Dixie* with our hamburgers and beer. Andy and Curtis were playing at the *Chicago Dance Palace* way down on South Jefferson Street. Because of the weather, more than any other reason, we had decided not to go there, and so we weren't in any hurry to finish our supper.

I noticed Cheechee peering out the window with a concerned stare, his entire body tense. Then I noticed the two people out on the sidewalk that had caught his attention; I could understand his concern. Johnny Dempsey and Tony Delaware paused in the entryway where the front door was recessed into the corner of the building, affording them some shelter from the light rainfall. I knew Tony had spotted us because we made direct eye contact as they passed by the window, but I wasn't certain that Johnny had noticed us. They talked for a bit, and then Tony patted his belly and pointed to the general direction of inside the *Dixie*. I supposed Tony was trying to convince Johnny that satisfying his hunger was top priority at the moment, but Johnny seemed more interested in moving on. Finally, Johnny walked off into the rainy night, and Tony pulled open the door. Cheechee relaxed and I saw relief in his eyes.

Tony invited himself to sit down at our table, and then as an afterthought he said, "You don't mind if I join you, do you?"

"Of course not," Cheechee instantly replied.

Despite a baseball cap and a light jacket, Tony was dripping from the rain. He took off his jacket and cap, leaned away from the table and ruffled his hair with both hands, shedding most of the wetness onto the floor. His hair stood out in all directions, but that's usually the way it was; I had never seen it neatly combed. After he ordered a hamburger and a beer, I sensed that there was something different about Tony that night. He was usually happy-go-lucky, always smiling, always ready for snappy conversation and willing to consider some suggested spring for a thrill. He was much like Cheechee except that he wasn't quite ready to give up his youthful, fun-loving ways; he wasn't yet ready to settle down or make any commitments.

That night, though, his spirit seemed dampened, but not from the rain. His perpetual smile was only half there and his usual vibrancy did not radiate as I had always seen before. I knew he had been hanging out with Johnny Dempsey a great deal, and I had even heard that since he came back from California he had been hanging his baseball cap at Johnny's place. I suspected he was experiencing the same kind of conflicts that Cheechee had, but I didn't know him all that well yet; I decided I would wait for him to volunteer whatever he wanted to tell.

"You still living with your Aunt?" Cheechee asked Tony.

Now, *that* was a brilliant question. Cheechee must've been reading my mind. He was probably just as curious as me, but he didn't want to probe too sharply into a personal matter.

"Yeah... well... no..." Tony was a little indecisive. "I've been stayin' at Johnny's place for a while."

"Oh," Cheechee said. "I stayed there for a while, too, but I didn't care for the neighborhood. Now I live with Andy and Will."

"I don't care much for the neighborhood, either," Tony responded. He winked at Cheechee and gave a little smirk, as if he thought he was hiding a personal joke between them.

"It's okay," Cheechee said. "Will knows."

From there, the conversation became a little more open. This was actually the first time I had ever talked to Tony outside the Lion's Den get-togethers. Here, away from that crowd of peers he seemed slightly more tranquil, although there was the possibility that he could've been under the influence of some drug that Johnny had provided.

"I had to get out of my Aunt's house... at least for a while," Tony explained. "Gertrude was just getting too damned controlling."

"Why do you live with your Aunt?" I asked. "Where are your folks?"

"They're both dead... in the graveyard at Bisbee, Arizona."

"Sorry," I said. "What happened?"

"They were prospectors... worked a little silver mine out in the desert hills where we lived. One day the rocks gave way and the mineshaft caved in on them. I was only nine. I rode our burrow twenty miles into Bisbee for help. But by the time anybody could dig them out, they were both goners.

"About a week after the funeral, the sheriff located my Aunt Gertrude in St. Louis, and she came out and took me back here. I guess if there is such a thing as culture shock for a kid of nine, it happened to me. I was used to the outdoor open air and the hot sun and the solitude of the desert, living in a two-room adobe. We went into town once a month for supplies. All of a sudden, I'm living in a big plush house in city environment, getting schooled by private tutors until I was ready to enter public school. It was quite an adjustment."

"Must've been a little overwhelming," I said.

"Especially at first," Tony went on. "I slowly got accustomed to the city life, but I still long for the outdoors. Now, Aunt Gertrude insists that I'm going to University."

"So, why did you go to Johnny's?" Cheechee asked.

"Aunt Gertrude knows all my other friends. It was the only place where I figured she wouldn't find me."

"And now you're not exactly happy at Johnny's?"

"He's smothering me, Cheechee. Johnny follows me every place I go. I can't go to the bathroom without him being right outside the door. He thinks I should be by his side night and day."

"What about tonight?"

"He had some *business* to do... you know... and I told him I'd meet him later."

"Why don't you just go back to your Aunt's house?"

"I talked to her, but now she's gettin' all pissy with me... said the next time I come to her house, it should only be to get my stuff out. Thinks I'm acting ungrateful."

I could see that an emotional disaster of some sort was inevitable, given the volatile atmosphere. "D'ya have any plans?" I asked.

Tony gazed at a far wall. "Farther than next Friday night... no. Got any suggestions?"

"D'ya have a job?"

He looked at me with sad eyes and shook his head.

"If you like the outdoors, you could try to get a job on the river."

Tony looked at me again, this time with curiosity. "What do you mean?"

"Riverboats. You might be able to get a job on a riverboat. Travel up and down the Mississippi. See lots of places. Find one you like, move there, and viola, you've solved all your problems."

"You make it sound so simple," Tony said. "I don't think it'll be that easy."

"Listen," Cheechee said. "That's a great idea. Will knows what he's talking about when it comes to riverboats. He and his brother owned one, and he lived and worked on the river for many years."

"Are you at least interested?" I asked Tony.

"Well... I don't know... maybe... sure, I'd give it a shot... but I really don't want to go back to Johnny's place tonight."

My eyes met Cheechee's, and I knew we were thinking the same thoughts. If we allowed Tony to come to our house, we could be compromising the security of our sanctuary—that place where we had been safe from the people we didn't want to find us. But it wouldn't be right to turn our backs on a friend, either.

CHAPTER FIFTEEN

SINCE Andy had recently moved into the bigger bedroom with Cheechee so Curtis could move from his downtown cracker box apartment into Andy's old room, Curtis was now an official member of our household; it seemed only fair that he should have a vote in the decision to offer Tony safe haven in our house. Neither he nor Andy displayed any objections. But Monday morning was the last morning that Tony ate breakfast with us. He understood our desire for our street address to remain unknown to Johnny Dempsey. Most grateful for our concern with his current situation, he knew, too, that if he accepted our offer of a *temporary* place to stay, Johnny might follow him here, and he sincerely didn't want to jeopardize our friendship in that way. He'd try to somehow work things out.

Tony bid us a farewell with the promise that no one would know where he had been for two nights. We wished him luck and assured him that we would still honor our offer to help if it became necessary.

After he left for the bus stop, everything seemed to be

back to normal.

"Now that we have a little break in our schedule," Andy announced, "I'm gonna take a bus to St. Charles to visit Mom for a few days. Wanna come along, Cheechee?"

"Not this time," Cheechee replied. "I've got a lot of writing to do. Will has stirred up some ideas in my head, and I want to write it down before I forget it."

"And I'm going to an estate sale over on the west end of town," Curtis said. "Will... d'ya wanna come with me?"

I wasn't exactly excited about going to look at some old dead guy's furniture and dishes. "No, but you can drop me off at Sadie's house. I promised her I'd work at the studio today for a few hours."

"It's a deal," Curtis said. "I can pick you up again on my way back."

We dropped Andy off at the bus depot to catch the 9:45 to St. Charles. Then Curtis drove me to Sadie's house. "I'll pick you up around three o'clock," he informed me.

"You really don't have to, y' know... I can catch a bus."

"Nonsense," Curtis scolded. "I'll be here about three."

Before I could say any more, he rattled away in his rusty old blue Ford sedan.

Sadie's studio was quite busy at this time of year with all the school graduations coming soon, confirmations, bar mitzvahs and June wedding announcements. There was plenty of work to keep me busy, and the day went by so quickly that I was surprised to see Curtis standing just inside the front entrance. I glanced at the clock; it was 3:15.

"If you're not ready to go, I can come back later," he said.

Sadie intervened. She was just finishing with her last client of the day. "You're already fifteen minutes past the time you said you would leave," she said with a big smile. "I'm almost done anyway." She insisted that Curtis should not have to make another trip.

I ran up the stairs to say good-bye to Philip, but the nanny winked and said she would be happy to relay the message when Master Philip awoke from his afternoon nap.

When we walked down the sidewalk to the street, I didn't see Curtis's car. "Where did you park?" I asked.

Curtis beamed a big toothy grin and pointed at the shiny two-tone red and maroon sedan parked right in front of me. "I bought it at the estate sale today," he said. "Saw it listed on the sale bill, so I thought I'd check it out. Guess I got lucky, 'cause nobody else was interested. And I needed a better car."

He was right about that; there were times that he and Andy walked part way home from a late night gig because the old car broke down. I sauntered around the shiny new machine as Curtis told me all about it. "1934 Pontiac... barely ever out of the garage, so it's practically still like new. The old guy croaked just after he bought it, and his wife couldn't drive, so it sat in the garage all this time until she died."

I opened the door and peered inside. The chrome-ringed gauges on the wood-grain dash sparkled in the sunlight. Rich brown mohair covered the seats that appeared as if they had never been sat on; even the floor mats looked as though they had never seen the sole of a dirty shoe. I was impressed. "Looks expensive," I said. But, of course, I knew Curtis and Andy were making a lot of money, and he could afford it.

"I paid half of what I expected... three hundred and twenty-five dollars for a car that sold new for eight seventy-five."

"What'd you do with your old car?"

"Sold it for ten dollars to a junk man who happened to be there."

"So," I said, grinning. "Are you gonna take me for a ride?"

"Hop in!"

CHAPTER SIXTEEN

ANDY was still in St. Charles on Wednesday and Cheechee was so busy writing that I think he forgot he needed to eat. He passed on a hamburger at the *Dixie*, seemingly happy with his box of crackers and cheese. Curtis and I went without him.

As the proud owner of a new car, Curtis wanted to take a little ride in the country before dark, so he headed across Eads Bridge to East St. Louis on the Illinois side of the river. We were all the way to Collinsville when he decided we should head back to our favorite supper spot. Curtis was an excellent driver, and I could tell he was in love with his new Pontiac... and for good reason; it was like riding in a dream compared to that rickety old jalopy he had before.

Dusk shrouded St. Louis when Curtis parked his snazzy

new car in front of the *Dixie*. Darkness would soon gobble up everything and bright lights would electrify the city. We made ourselves comfortable at our usual table in the corner by the window, and now it served a double purpose: Curtis could stare out the window at his new love, *his* Pontiac.

We had been there a while when Tony showed up. He'd checked here often hoping to find us. "Where's Cheechee?" he asked, as if he was surprised that I was there without him.

"He's at home working on his book," I said.

"Oh. Well, it's you I wanted to talk to, anyway." Tony appeared in better spirits now than when we had last seen him. His energetic smile was back. His clothes were fresh and clean. His hair still stood out in all directions, but that was to be expected; that's what made him *Tony*.

"I managed to talk to Aunt Gertrude," he began. "I spent all day after I left your place planning what I would say to her, and I practiced saying it over and over to a tree in the park."

"And how did that turn out?"

"I gave her my deepest regrets and most sincere apologies for appearing disrespectful, but I also explained that the University stuff was just too overwhelming right now... that I wasn't ready for that yet."

"Did she understand?"

"I think so... at least she's letting me come back to live in her house again... for the time being, anyway."

"Well, that's great, Tony," I said, showing as much encouragement as I could muster. "Sounds like you've licked the problem."

"That's not all," Tony added. "I worked things out with Johnny, too."

"Oh? What did you work out with him?"

"I told him that we could still be friends, but that I couldn't be with him twenty-four hours a day, every day. I told him that I have my own life to live, that I was moving back to my Aunt's house, and if he promised not to follow me around everywhere I went, or make trouble for me when I'm with other friends, I would still come to see him once in a while."

"And will you?"

"Yeah... well... maybe."

Curtis joined in. "Think that's a good idea? Johnny is—"

"Johnny's okay... he's just a little overbearing sometimes."

To me it sounded as if Tony might be headed in the right direction, but he was still indecisive on his opinion of Johnny Dempsey. He could still be lured by a bad influence, but I didn't think it was my place to tell him that I thought Johnny was a bad influence.

"There's something else that I wanted to talk to you about, Will," Tony continued.

"What about?" I said.

"The other night you said I could get a job on a riverboat."

"Yeah, I think you prob'ly could."

"Would you help me with that?"

If there was any one subject that I could coach, it would be life aboard a riverboat. In the last five years, I had spent more time afloat with wooden decks beneath my feet than I had on solid, dry earth. Although the times were changing— diesel engine power was slowly replacing steam—from what I had gathered from Jesse on his not-so-frequent days at home, the protocol had not changed. Navigation on the big river was the same now as it had been for many years, except on the Upper Mississippi the Army Corp of Engineers had built several dams and locks, and construction of more was in progress. As far as the crew was concerned, their duties were still the same; only one job would have been eliminated on a diesel powered boat—the fireman. No one would be shoveling coal into a boiler firebox. But deckhands are still deckhands; engineers still run the engine room; cabin boys are still cabin boys; cooks and their helpers still prepare the food; the pilot still steers the boat, and the Captain and his Mate still oversee the whole operation. No, not much had changed since I stepped off the Madison.

I sensed that Tony might be serious about working on the river, and I could think of no reason to discourage him.

"Meet me here tomorrow at ten o'clock," I told Tony. "We'll talk about it, and then we'll go down to the levee."

CHAPTER SEVENTEEN

I SPENT the entire next day with Tony acclimating him to the river and the big boats, explaining protocol and teaching him the terminology, the "river lingo" he needed to know. We even came across a couple of Captains who remembered me, and they allowed me to take Tony aboard their vessels to show him around. By late afternoon I had put him in contact with several Captains and First Mates, plus a list of others that weren't in port but would be within the next week or so. Tony seemed enthusiastic, and when Aaron Tyler, the First Mate on the Hercules asked if I was interested in joining his crew, because he was quite familiar with the Madison, I thought Tony would throw me overboard when I replied, "I don't think I'm quite ready to go back on the river yet. Let me think it over."

I know Tony would've felt more comfortable working with me there, and maybe I shouldn't have acted so selfishly. Maybe I should have taken Mr. Tyler up on his offer, and Tony would've been hired on the spot, too.

But I *wasn't* ready. I had dabbled in photography and I wanted to see where it might take me. I was still young enough to try new things, and then return to the river at my choosing. And besides, I had made my commitment to Big Brother Jesse the day we lost our boat, and I owed my loyalty to him. In the deep, dark reaches of my mind, I knew it was doubtful that our old crew—Jesse, Luke, Reggie, Andy and me—would ever be back together again, but I wanted to hold onto that hope for all it was worth. Although I had made many new friends in St. Louis, I missed the old ones.

Cheechee was already home when I got there, bathed squeaky clean and clad in a freshly-laundered white *Arrow* dress shirt, tailored so nicely that it made him look like a young executive. But his emotion didn't match the stunning attire as he sat at the writing desk staring blankly into his notebook.

"Curtis is gonna drive me to the bus station," he said, but there was little of the usual cheerfulness in his voice. "Andy is coming back from St. Charles on the six-fifteen."

I knew immediately that something was troubling him. "What's wrong?" I said. "Aren't you happy that Andy's back?"

"Of course I'm happy he's back... but I have some bad news."

"What—?"

"The warehouse supervisor cut my hours down to just two days a week."

Although it did sound rather devastating, I tried to ease the pain. "Well, that's not so terrible... at least you still *have* a job. That's better than a lot of people these days."

"I guess so," he replied. "But now I'll be making less than half of what I was... and that's not much."

Of all of us, Cheechee was categorically the least prepared to lose his income, although he had not totally lost it yet. It would certainly put a strain on his expendable cash, but I knew that Andy would never let him starve or sleep on a park bench under a newspaper salvaged from the trash barrel. Nor would I. Cheechee was a part of *my* family now, too, just as equally as Andy, Jesse, Luke, Reggie, Sadie, Philip... and I'd put Curtis in the circle, too, even though he could be a bit ec-centric at times, wildly extravagant—like buying a flashy red car—but he, too, was focused on camaraderie, and I'd bet that he'd go down fighting for any one of us. I felt confident that Cheechee was in good company, and he had nothing to fear.

I put a hand on his shoulder. "Don't worry, Cheechee," I said. "You're among brothers that aren't going to let anything happen. We'll all get through it together."

He jumped up from the chair and threw his arms around me in an affectionate bear hug like Big Brother Jesse always did. "Thanks, Will," is all he said right then, and I knew he meant it. Nothing else was necessary.

"Who wants to come along to the bus station?" Curtis called out as he came in from the back yard. He'd been washing his car. Cheechee had gained his composure by then and we were sitting on the parlor couch. When Curtis saw the solemn mood he said, "Did Cheechee tell you about his job?"

We both nodded.

"I told him not to worry," Curtis said. "We're all here to help each other."

"See?" I said to Cheechee, and I caught a fraction of a grin creep onto his gloomy face. "Everything will be okay here."

Sorrow had sort of ruined Cheechee's excitement for the grand surprise he had planned for me. Little had I known earlier in the week that he was feverishly preparing a fresh, clean copy of the manuscript—or as much of it as he wanted me to see now—that he had been working on all winter. He stepped over to the writing desk, picked up the notebook, and then gingerly handed it to me. Neatly printed in big, bold letters on the front cover was:

IF I COULD STEAL THE STARS
by Christopher Chapman

"I know you read a lot," he told me. "So... you can tell me if it's any good. Read it at your leisure, but *please* don't give it to anyone else… and for God's sake don't discuss it with anybody, okay?"

It was true. I did read a lot. Cheechee had seen the accumulation of books lining the shelves in my room, and he'd even borrowed a few.

"You have my word," I assured him.

I would have let Curtis and Cheechee go to the bus station while I prepared a good supper for all of us, but they insisted that I come along, and then we could all go to the *Dixie* for hamburgers and beer. In light of Cheechee's situation, it was probably a good idea. In light of Curtis celebrating his new car, it was a *very* good idea. In light of the fact that I didn't really feel like cooking, anyway, it was a *great* idea.

Andy was just as surprised with the new red Pontiac as any of us. He stared at Cheechee with a devious, questioning grin.

"I didn't have a thing to do with it!" Cheechee said. "Curtis bought and *paid* for this car himself!"

We all had a good laugh, and then we climbed into the new red Pontiac; Curtis drove us to the best hamburgers in all of St. Louis. Andy was glad to be back, and he was quite pleased with the new car; no more walking home in the middle of the night from a broken down jalopy.

He told me about his visit in St. Charles, and in particular, about his visit to Spades Morgan. "He has a stateroom on the *Goldenrod* now, and I just caught him before he left for New Orleans." Cheechee knew about Spades, but Curtis didn't, so there followed a brief explanation about Andy's real father, and my connection to him, as well.

I told Andy about Tony and how I set him up with contacts to hire on with riverboat crews. "I got a job offer, too, from First Mate Aaron Tyler on the Hercules."

"You gonna take it?" Andy asked.

"No."

"Will! Why not? The Hercules is a *great* boat."

"I know. I'm just not ready yet. I wanna wait to see what Jesse does."

"But that could be months—"

"I know... but I'll wait."

Then the conversation turned to Curtis. "Hear anything from Harry?" Andy asked him.

"Not a word, so far. Looks like we've got the weekend off."

CHAPTER EIGHTEEN

DURING the next few weeks, Andy and Curtis played a pretty light schedule at the theaters and clubs. I thought they were lowering their standards when they started performing at neighborhood bars, but as they kept telling me, it didn't matter *where* they played as long as the money kept coming in.

Because Cheechee was only working two days a week, he started singing along at their practice sessions. He knew the words to many of the songs they played only instrumentally. At first they were just having fun, but then it seemed as though they had discovered a wild card in Cheechee's voice; the *trio* began working in earnest, and before long there was a whole new versatility in their music. I had always known of Andy's talent, and practically the entire city of St. Louis had confirmed that he and Curtis, together, were quite sensational. Now, with Cheechee's rich tenor voice added, St. Louis was in for another new treat. Even *my* limited knowledge of music skills could identify the potential.

Cheechee was a little nervous about performing in front of a real audience; Curtis suggested that for the first couple appearances, scheduled weeks earlier, Cheechee could join them on stage part-way into the show after the audience was "warmed up." He could sing one song, or as many as he felt comfortable with. "But you'll be fine once you get started... you'll see," Curtis said.

"Maybe," Cheechee replied. "But I always sang with a group, y' know, the school choir and such. Never sang solo before... not for a big audience."

"You won't be alone," Andy assured him. "Curtis and I will be right there with you."

Sadie's studio had remained fairly busy all along, so naturally I stayed busy, too. I went to bed every night at a reasonable hour so that I might be fresh and alert at the studio, but the night that Cheechee made his debut as the new voice of The Gaslight Knights, I couldn't just stay at home. They were playing at a place called Charlie's, a combination bar and dance hall, way out on the west end of the city. The warm April weather enticed people out of their houses, and Charlie's Place certainly did a good job of luring them in. When we arrived a little before nine that Friday night, the parking lot was nearly full. The crowd inside was already primed with alcohol, and I could feel the pent-up energy among them waiting to be unleashed.

Andy and Curtis started playing while Cheechee stayed with me for a while, perhaps to build his courage after seeing the enormous crowd he would have to face. We sipped cold beers, mingled with the noisy horde and looked for any familiar faces, to no avail. There were plenty of people seemingly more interested in getting intoxicated than they were in music and dancing, but the dance floor was full of bodies, too, all moving in one big mass. The Gaslight Knights were sufficiently satisfying.

About a half-hour into their show I saw Curtis waving and motioning for Cheechee to come up onto the stage. "Ladies and gentlemen," he spoke into the microphone. "We have a surprise for you tonight."

The crowd quieted a little with curious stares as the crisp white shirt approached the microphone and came to rest beside Curtis. "Making his first public singing appearance tonight, please welcome Cheechee..." He stepped back, and on cue, he and Andy began the introduction to Cheechee's first number, *I Get a Kick Out of You,* a song that had been made quite popular by Paul Whiteman last December. A few hands clapped, a couple of whoops were heard, and a whistle or two sounded.

It wasn't difficult to see that Cheechee was jittery, but he started singing to the now subdued audience in his vibrant style. As the crowd gradually gained its momentum once again, apparently in approval and acceptance of the new voice singing one of their favorite songs, I could see Cheechee's tension dissolving. By the time he sang his second and third songs, the audience had decided they liked this dazzling new talent. Later, when he finished his night with *My Little Grass Shack in Kealakekua, Hawaii* they were chanting *"Chee-Chee, Chee-Chee, Chee-Chee."* Thanks to Andy and Curtis, Christopher Chapman had taken his first step into show business, and I had recorded it on film.

This was a less sophisticated crowd than I had seen at the *Arcadia*, and I sincerely hoped all the energy would be contained on the dance floor. But typical of any large gathering where the liquor took control of a few who didn't know when they'd had enough, about midnight the place turned into a brawling pandemonium. It started among a group near the bar, and at first I thought that's where it would stay. Next thing I knew, though, like an infectious disease it spread quickly throughout the barroom. Try as I might to avoid any contact, the side of my face caught a wild flying fist that I doubt was intended for me. A fighter, I was not. Without mounting any retaliation, I just scrambled to get away and managed to find the exit before any more violence found me, or my *Leica* got smashed. Curtis's Pontiac was across the parking lot, and I thought that would be the safest place to wait out the mayhem. I sat on the running board of the locked car until Curtis, Andy, and Cheechee showed up a half-hour later. Apparently, Cheechee had been accosted as well; the sleeve of his new $2.50 *Arrow* white shirt was nearly ripped off, but otherwise they all seemed to have escaped unscathed.

"We were worried about you," Cheechee said. "I went out looking for you... that's when some roughneck grabbed me and tore my shirt." Then he caught a glimpse of the dandy bruise on the side of my face. "What happened to you?" he said. In the dark parking lot I hadn't been able to see my reflection in the car window well enough, but the wound obviously looked worse than I had imagined. Andy and Cheechee fussed over me while Curtis unlocked the doors and put his saxophone case in the back.

"I'm okay!" I insisted. "It's not like I'm crippled or something." Their concern and attention, though, did make me feel good.

On the ride home Curtis nudged my arm. "Y' know the best part?" he said. "When the owner of the place came to pay us our forty bucks by the back door, he gave us an extra ten bucks... said he hadn't seen such a rambunctious crowd all winter... said we could come back anytime we wanted."

That was the first of many engagements at various neighborhood bars and taverns that ended in a late-night free-for-all or a parking lot rumble that often entailed bloodshed. I didn't see them all, but I heard about them. What a way for Cheechee to start his show biz career!

CHAPTER NINETEEN

TOO embarrassed about the unsightly contusion on my face to let Sadie see it, I begged off work for a few days, telling her on the telephone that I wasn't feeling well. I hoped that the swelling and the brilliant purple color would dissipate soon.

"Should I come over to look in on you?" she asked.

"NO!" I responded hastily, and then I restated my answer in a calmer tone, to make her not believe that I was trying to hide something. "No, there's no need for that. You're busy, and besides... Curtis and Andy and Cheechee are here... they won't let me die."

"Should I send my doctor over to see you?"

"No, Sadie. That won't be necessary. I just have a little stomach flu, that's all. I'll be fine in a few days."

She knew how close Jesse and I were and I was afraid that she would come anyway. I thought the world of her, just as I did Jesse, but this was one time when I wished she would stay away, so that I wouldn't have to explain that I got in the middle of a barroom brawl.

Monday afternoon I settled down on the parlor couch with Cheechee's manuscript, *If I Could Steal the Stars*, and I read a couple of pages. It began:

> *Sometimes my mind drifts back to a time that per-haps went by too quickly. Then, I was wishing to grow older. Now, I live to stay young and not to die. If I could just steal all the stars from the sky, time would stop, and I could stay a kid forever.*

I thought about that for a few moments; what a profound statement! It had the ring of a seasoned philosopher, yet it sounded like the voice of an innocent child. If I didn't already know the author, I wouldn't have pictured Cheechee.

I read on, discovering that the first part was a brief summary of someone's early life, progressing quickly into his teen years. I could only assume that Cheechee was describing his own existence, as I had suspected this would be. But then I read the passage that said he really liked his dad, and that he had so many fond memories of him. To me, this seemed odd, because I had been given the impression that Cheechee's father was a disgusting drunkard that couldn't take care of his family. But then I read some more. The summary raced from grammar school and playing baseball in a sandlot, to stealing a car and reform school. Now, that sounded more like Cheechee.

> *There came a point in my life that I was not comfortable with the restrictions that society placed on me... I played beyond the limits that were socially accepted...*

I heard a knock on the front door, abruptly closed the notebook and thought of running upstairs to lock myself in my room. But Andy's footsteps rushed to the door too quickly. There was no time. I was caught. Sadie was going to see my black-and-blue face.

"Yeah, he's in the parlor," I heard Andy say cheerfully. "He'll be glad to see you."

I wouldn't have been happy to see *Will Rogers* right then, but I got up to bravely face... "JESSE!" Suddenly I forgot about my bruised cheek and dashed to the door.

"I just got home this morning," Jesse said. "Sadie told me to come over here, that you were sick..." He studied my face for a long moment. "Good heavens, Little Brother! What happened to you?"

It never crossed my mind that I should be ashamed to tell Jesse the truth about what had really happened. We'd never kept secrets from each other, and I certainly wasn't shy about admitting to him that I was at a rowdy bar and got clobbered by some drunk who missed his intended target and hit me instead. "I didn't want to tell Sadie... thought she'd think badly of me... and I didn't want to show up at the studio looking like this."

"I wouldn't worry about that," Jesse said laughing. He seemed to be amused by the whole situation. "Why were you at a roughneck bar like that, anyhow?"

"Andy and Curtis were playing there... and Cheechee sings with them now, too. It was his first time on stage, so I *had* to go... to take pictures."

"You should've seen it, Jesse," Andy bragged. "Will flattened that guy with one punch!"

Jesse ruffled my hair like he always did. "Way to go, Little Brother."

"No, no, no, Jesse," I said laughing. "It didn't happen that way. I cleared outa there before I got clobbered again. Those guys were more than *twice* my size."

"Well, I guess that was the smart thing to do," Jesse said.

By then, Curtis and Cheechee had joined us, too. Even though they had only met Jesse at Christmastime, they considered him a close friend, and they were glad to see him.

"Hey, Cheechee," Jesse said. "Will tells me you're singing with Andy and Curtis now."

"Yeah," Cheechee replied. "Came at the right time, too, 'cause I'm losing my job at the warehouse."

"Sorry to hear that."

"It's okay... I like show biz better. It pays more."

"Say..." Jesse turned to me again. "You'll never guess who I ran into down in Natchez last week," he said. I could tell he was quite amused with this bit of information, too.

"Spades Morgan?" I said. It was a good guess, because Andy had told me Spades was traveling south.

"Well, I saw him, too, down in Baton Rouge a couple of weeks ago."

"So who did you see in Natchez?" Andy asked.

"J.D. McDermott."

My lower jaw bounced off my breastbone. "Then, he didn't drown," I mumbled.

Jesse eyed me suspiciously.

"Did he remember you?" I asked.

"He did," Jesse replied. "Said he fell overboard off our boat that night the band was playing so loud. No one heard him yelling for help. He was stranded on a sandbar 'til the next morning when another boat picked him up and took him all the way to New Orleans."

Curtis and Cheechee didn't have a clue about what we were discussing, but Andy had been filled in on the whole story about McDermott winning our riverboat in a poker game—before it was *our* boat—and Spades Morgan winning it back. Andy also knew about McDermott and Spades facing off on the Texas deck of the Madison that night, with me watching, in a confrontation over a murder that Spades saw McDermott commit ten years prior. McDermott fell overboard as a result of his own guilty conscience. But there was so much hatred toward McDermott that Morgan and I pretended we knew nothing about it when McDermott turned up missing.

"Did you know he fell overboard?" Jesse asked.

"N-no... Spades said something about... um... no I didn't."

I guess, now, I should retract my statement about *never*

keeping a secret from my Big Brother Jesse. But I think that's the *only* one.

We all talked and had a grand time the rest of the afternoon, and, of course, Curtis had to show Jesse his new Pontiac.

"Luke should see it," Jesse said. "He's thinking about a car."

"What about Reggie?" I asked. "What's he doing now?"

"Reggie got a job as a salesman at a clothing store downtown... the Top Hat. You should stop in and see him."

"I will." I couldn't imagine Reggie dressed in a salesman's suit and tie in a fancy store like the Top Hat, but his British accent and his flair of sophistication would fit right in.

About four o'clock, Jesse indicated that he should be going. "Our boat is getting some repairs, and Luke and I have some classes to attend, so we'll be in town for a few days."

"Classes?"

"Yeah... I'm getting my pilot's license, too," Jesse said.

"That's great! How long 'til you get your command?"

"Could be as far off as next year, Will. They're a lot more stringent about training pilots now."

Maybe some things on the river *had* changed.

CHAPTER TWENTY

AFTER a couple of days the swelling was gone from my cheek, but there still remained a little discoloration of the skin. Although I still didn't want to go to the studio in that condition, it wasn't so bad that I couldn't go downtown.

"I'm gonna take the bus downtown," I announced. "Wanna come with me, Andy?"

"What are you going to do?" Andy asked.

"Look up Reggie."

"Sure, I'll come. I'd like to see Reggie again, too."

Cheechee overheard our conversation and popped his head around the corner. "Are you going to that Top Hat clothing store?"

"Yeah, if we can find it."

"I know right where it is," Cheechee said. "That's where I bought my new white shirt that got wrecked. I need a new one, so I'll go too... if you don't mind."

Curtis called out from the kitchen, "What's this I hear about you taking the bus downtown?"

"We're going down to the Top Hat Clothier," Andy replied.

"On the bus?"

"Yeah."

"Nonsense! I'll drive you downtown in the car."

Curtis was always ready and willing to play chauffeur with his new red Pontiac. And the rest of us were always ready and willing to let him.

On the way into town, we were all in agreement that cer-

tain articles of clothing were needed by each of us, and because Reggie was probably earning some sort of commission
on his sales, we would all purchase something from him. I
certainly needed a new pair of trousers; Cheechee needed a
shirt; Andy said he could use some new socks and underwear; and Curtis was in the market for a new hat *and* trousers. There would be no better place to get them.

Curtis parked his car in the nearest parking lot about four
blocks away from the Top Hat. We didn't mind the walk on
that pleasantly warm spring day. We passed more than a
dozen out-of-work men selling apples on the street corners,
and I could only imagine that come nightfall, they would all
be standing in some breadline. My heart went out to them as
I stopped to buy an apple, not from just one, but three different men. Their expressions were so grateful when I handed
over the nickels; it was quite gratifying to me. Then Curtis
and Andy followed my lead, and they purchased a couple of
apples each, and finally Cheechee decided that he should afford himself just one. But his heart was in the right place.

We noticed that there appeared to be more people just
walking aimlessly about; farmers had lost their land to fore-
closure; city dwellers were unable to find jobs when factories
shut down all production. Few businesses remained flush,
some had closed their doors, and many more were merely
operating on a shoestring. President Franklin D. Roosevelt
had improved the nation's condition   after entering the
White House in 1933 with his "New Deal" that created gov-
ernment work forces, providing jobs for some. But there
were mixed emotions among the people; some still support-
ed him strongly, while others opposed. He was up for re-
election, and only time would tell the rest of the story.

We walked the remaining distance slowly, eating our apples while we contemplated our fortunate position in this
ailing society. *Where would it all end?* we wondered, and we

recognized that we could only live day-by-day, keeping our-selves focused on survival.

But so far, we *had* survived the Depression's revolting blows. Perhaps we *were* lucky. Perhaps we *had* fallen into the right hands at the right time. But it wasn't *all luck.* We had faced the adversities with strong will and healthy body, and we had persevered and maintained our hold on whatev-er we had. No, it wasn't *all* just luck.

We entered the Top Hat, a large, classy, men's clothier, ex-pecting to find a rampantly busy atmosphere. But it was something less than rampant. At the very center of the store, an escalator made its silent, resolute movement upward, and likewise, beside it a column of steps came steadily, silently down. Neither column carried a single soul. Row upon row of racks and aisle after aisle of gondolas contained every piece of men's clothing and accessories imaginable, being scrutinized by only a very few potential customers.

Just inside the door we were greeted by a distinguished gentleman, dark blue business suit, starched white shirt and tie. "May I be of assistance?" he said politely.

"Yes, actually," I replied. "I would like to see the salesman named Reginald Peirce. Is he here today?"

"Certainly," the suited man said. "I'll get him for you." He turned and walked toward the back of the store.

A couple of minutes later, our foursome had dispersed in-to the immediate area viewing various textile items. When Reggie saw us, he practically ran up the aisle to meet us, grinning.

"Will, Andy," he said, seemingly overwhelmed by our presence. "It's so bloody great to see you." He looked rather stunning in his blue suit, starched shirt and tie. He gave us all hearty handshakes. "What brings you here?"

"Well, actually, we came to see you," I started. "But we came to buy some clothes, too."

"You came to the right place..."

We chatted briefly about our present situations, and then, because Reggie's supervisor was apparently monitoring his activity, he shifted into salesman high gear. "So, what can I help you find?"

We expressed our needs and Reggie guided each of us to the various departments of goods. He expertly measured across Cheechee's broad shoulders, and then stretched the tape down the length of his arm to determine proper shirt size, pointing out the racks with the "perfect fit" shirts for Cheechee.

Then he put his tape around my waist and measured my inseam. "Will... looks like you've put on a little weight since I saw you last," he said smiling, and proceeded to show me dozens of trousers in my size.

When he was finished with all of us, we couldn't have been more satisfied. Everything was of perfect fit and color.

"I wish we had more time to talk," I told Reggie when we were about to leave. "Maybe you could meet us some night at the *Dixie*. You remember that place?"

"Sure," Reggie said. "Jesse used to take us there. It's on Pine Street, is it not?"

"That's the place. We'll have supper there some night. I'll let you know when."

CHAPTER TWENTY-ONE

WE made good our promise to Reggie the following week. I had gone back to work at Sadie's studio when the black-and-blue was hardly noticeable. (Sadie only asked if I was feeling better, so I trust that Jesse didn't tell her about the bar fight.) When I knew that Jesse and Luke were back on the river again, there seemed little chance that Reggie would be preoccupied, so we arranged to meet at the *Dixie* Thursday evening after he was through with work.

Andy and I had a ball reminiscing the good old times on the Madison with Reggie. He'd get us going with "Remember that time when..." and we'd recall incidents like the time the new pilot ran us aground in the fog; or the time we captured the "river pirates" in the coal bin; or the time someone cut our mooring lines and we were adrift alone down the Missouri River in the middle of the night. We carried on for several hours, every once in a while stopping to explain something that Cheechee and Curtis couldn't understand without explanation. I think Cheechee was taking mental notes for his next book; Curtis was just plain entertained.

I got the impression that Reggie wasn't enjoying his stay in St. Louis to its fullest, that he was spending much of his time alone. So I was glad that Reggie, Curtis, and Cheechee had the chance to spend some time together and get to know one another better. It helped broaden the scope of our circle, and it offered Reggie some needed companionship. He welcomed the idea that we should do this every week. And we did.

Summer burst into full bloom during May; even the nights were warm enough for outdoor activities. But I had been interrupted during several attempts to read Cheechee's manuscript, and I was determined to finish it—not only to satisfy his desire for feedback, but to satisfy my curiosity about his history, if this was in fact a true accounting of his life experiences. So one Saturday night when Andy, Curtis and Cheechee were out being The Gaslight Knights at some club, I settled in with Cheechee's notebook.

If I Could Steal the Stars was a touching story about a young boy growing up in Denver, Colorado. It didn't really have a plot, but there was so much feeling it didn't need one. It told of the boy's struggle, continually bullied by an older brother. His only escape, at times, was to slip away and hide under a railroad trestle. He played baseball in a sandlot with other neighborhood boys, but because he was younger and smaller than most of them, he was never able to score a run, much less, make it to first base.

His mother's passing seemed to be a turning point in his life. At age ten, his home became flophouses on Larimer Street because his father could afford no more. Dad had always liked the bottle, but losing his wife pushed him over the edge. His employer soon lost patience, and Dad soon lost his job.

It was after several months in a flophouse when the boy came to understand the reason for older brother Robert's animosity toward him: the younger boy was and always had been Dad's favorite son, and Big Brother's easy retaliation was mean treatment of Little Brother. But he eventually left to join a band of petty thieves in Greely.

No wonder the boy never stopped loving Dad; for the story went on to tell of walks in the mountain forest, fishing at a creek, and sometimes just a lazy Sunday in a park, all by

Dad's side. There seemed to be so much love and affection between them.

And then there came the hobo trip to Texas one summer, riding box cars, working carnivals, picking cucumbers, meeting interesting people. But the most heart-wrenching episode was Dad and Son accidentally getting separated for a day and a night. Tears streamed down my cheeks as I read it, and joy filled my heart when they were reunited by a stroke of luck.

Back in Denver, as the boy grew older and stronger, he was tempted by peers with illicit "fun," and his days of innocent childhood play was over. After a generous taste of uninhibited sex, drugs, and wild adventure, he was no longer satisfied with what society deemed acceptable. He stole a car so he and his buddies could go for a joy ride. That led to another, and another... and then his life seemed to be tethered to a revolving door in and out of jail and reform school until he became an "adult."

Another turning point occurred: he recognized his intelligence and talents; he woke up to realize his life, at this point, was a moralistic wreck. His father had become an invalid in a state asylum and now the boy's life in Denver was headed nowhere. One last deviant act got him a car that afforded him quick escape, which he abandoned a few miles from the city where it would easily be found and returned to its rightful owner. From there he hitchhiked across country to St. Louis, taking the time to reflect on his past, and to find a new sense of direction. In St. Louis, he would start over, and maybe there he would find a way to steal all the stars.

The story ended there, but somehow I knew that Cheechee intended to continue; too many things were still left unsaid.

The Gaslight Knights returned home long after I had gone

to bed; I didn't even hear them come in. The next morning they didn't wake up so early; they'd had a rough night at a dance hall in North St. Louis where several fights broke out at various times while they played. At the end of the dance, the final clash continued in the parking lot; Cheechee and Andy both had black eyes, and Curtis suffered some nasty bruises on his shoulders and one leg. They hadn't been able to avoid it, caught by surprise on their way to the car.

Although this was the first time they had suffered injuries, they had experienced other similar incidents; it was becoming discouraging. Harry hadn't gotten them into any of the respectable theaters for many weeks.

"Maybe we should just get out of St. Louis," Curtis suggested. "Try some other cities."

We all agreed that St. Louis was getting rough. Was it because the city was attracting so many out-of-work people? We didn't know, but there would be time to contemplate other options; Andy or Cheechee didn't want to perform in public with black eyes.

I sat on the back porch with Cheechee one afternoon while Andy and Curtis were practicing. "I've read your entire manuscript," I said. "I think it's very good, so far."

"Thanks, Will," Cheechee replied.

"But do you mind if I ask you one question?"

"Please, do."

"In your story, you say that you really liked your dad, but I thought you told us he was a drunk, and that he couldn't take care of you. Which is true?"

"Will, my father's an *alcoholic*... that's what I told you. It's true that he hasn't worked all the time. But I never said that I hate him."

"I'm sorry, Cheechee. Guess I must've misunderstood."

"Easy thing to do sometimes."

CHAPTER TWENTY-TWO

A FEW days later, near the end of May, we were all getting restless. Maybe it was just spring fever, but there seemed to be something else in the air, something unsettling that none of us recognized or could clarify. With the exception of—perhaps—Cheechee, we were all fairly financially secure, considering the economic times, and since he had started performing with Andy and Curtis, even Cheechee wasn't in any immediate danger of starvation. So, we knew money wasn't necessarily the issue. Curtis, Andy and Cheechee had discussed the possibility of playing at theaters and clubs in other cities, but so far there were no steadfast plans in place. The dread of finding more of the same violent audiences usually quenched the conversation.

While the black eyes and bruises healed, we needed some diversion to ease the anxiety. Andy and I had always enjoyed the cinema, so we drug Cheechee and Curtis to the movie theaters. Of course, they both admitted that they, too, were fans of the big screen, so it wasn't as if we were torturing them. We were thrilled with the high seas adventure of Captain Bligh and Fletcher Christian in *Mutiny on the Bounty;* we sat on the edge of our seats watching *The Bride of Frankenstein.* Curtis and Cheechee really enjoyed *Top Hat* starring Fred Astaire and Ginger Rogers, the song and dance musical that kept us laughing and smiling.

The Scarlet Empress was a tragedy and a farce all rolled into one baffling mess about a Russian princess, Sophia. We didn't know whether we should laugh or cry, and neither did the rest of the audience. No doubt, that movie was destined to be a box office flop. But we had no trouble laughing out loud at Clark Gable's gangster impression and Claudette Colbert's show-a-little-thigh hitch-hiking lesson in *It Happened One Night,* the motion picture that became the biggest hit of the year.

In the darkness of the theater we found reality in imagination, free from restrictions of real life. Ocean waves and spooky mansions, ten gallon hats and Colt .45s, flashy motorcars and raging stallions; they all passed through the screen from that wonderful world of cinema.

I awoke later than usual Monday morning after a late-night movie at the *Orpheum.* No one else was up yet, either. I stared at the calendar on the wall as I waited for the coffee to brew; it was June 3rd. I had informed Sadie that I planned to look up my friend, Keith Blake, the *St. Louis Post Dispatch* photographer who I had met the night Andy and Curtis opened for Benny Goodman at the Arcadia. Not that I expected to get a job with the newspaper, but Blake had told me to look him up sometime, and he would show me around, maybe put me in touch with the right people. It couldn't hurt.

I poured a cup of coffee to take to the back porch; that's where I most enjoyed my morning coffee now that the weather was warm. As I approached the door, I was startled by the sight of someone sitting on our back steps. He had his back to me, leaning against the railing, arms limp at his sides; he appeared to be asleep. I opened the door, thinking the noise would alert whoever it was of my presence, but it did not. I cautiously stepped closer to identify the sleeping stranger. But to my astonishment, it was not a stranger.

Tony Delaware's appearance was dismal, to say the least. His clothes were a mess—shirt stained and wrinkled; trousers caked with mud—his hair was dirty and mussed up more than usual, and his face was smeared and smudged from wiping it with soiled hands.

I stood there, gawking at Tony for a few moments, wondering what circumstance would have put him in that condition. A beating didn't seem likely because there appeared to be no cuts, scrapes or bruises. Likewise, he'd not fallen nor was he the victim of some accident. Physically he didn't look harmed.

I gently shook his shoulder. "Tony. Wake up," I said softly, as not to startle him.

His head jerked up and his whole body tensed, one hand grabbing for my wrist. His expression at first was that of fright, and then when he recognized who had wakened him, it turned to relief. "Will," he whispered.

"How long have you been out here?" I asked.

"Since dawn," he replied, his voice still raspy and weak. "I... I... I walked from the river last night... to the park... and I slept there for a while. Then just before sunup... I came here."

"What happened to you? Why are you so dirty?"

Tony gazed deeply, silently, into my eyes, and then tears spilled from his eyes, streaking down his dirty face. He buried his face in his hands, slumped, unable to speak.

I tried to coax some more out of him, but the only response from Tony was intense sobbing. I rubbed his shoulders and back, and it must have been comforting to him as it seemed to calm him a little, but I still couldn't get him to talk.

After some effort I finally helped him to stand. "Let's go inside," I said. "I've got fresh coffee in the pot. Would you like a cup of hot coffee?"

Tony nodded his approval, but still no words. Whatever happened to him had temporarily destroyed his ability to function wholly. Although I noticed no physical trauma, his endurance was nearly nonexistent as I assisted him into the kitchen and sat him down on a chair at the table. I poured another cup of coffee for him; his hand shook and he could barely raise the cup to his lips.

I just sat there with him, sipping my coffee, waiting for him to gain some strength. "Whenever you're ready to talk," I said as soothingly as I knew how, "I'm here to listen."

I heard Curtis stirring upstairs. I knew it was Curtis because his was the only room in the house that the floorboards squeaked when he walked across them. When he had made a brief visit to the bathroom, he came down to the kitchen. "I smell fresh coffee..." he said, and then he saw Tony in his miserable state. "Tony!" He obviously sensed that something was terribly wrong, and he just stared at me questioningly.

"I don't know," I said. "He's not saying anything. All I know is that he walked here from the river last night and slept in the park."

Tony continued his distant gaze and occasionally sipped his coffee. Nearly an hour later, he had not spoken a single word. Curtis suggested that we get him upstairs. "A warm bath and some clean clothes might help him feel better," he said.

I thought it sounded like an excellent idea. "How 'bout it, Tony? Does that sound agreeable to you?"

Tony glanced down at his filthy clothes and nodded.

He had stayed with us a couple of nights once before, so he was in familiar surroundings. That made it a simple matter to guide him up to the bathroom. I filled the tub while Curtis helped Tony get undressed. We both steadied him when he stepped into the bath and then stretched out in the warm, soothing water. Curtis soaped a washcloth and gently started scrubbing the grime from Tony's face and neck.

"You look like you've had some experience with that," I said to Curtis.

"When I was growing up," he replied, "I took care of three

little brothers that knew how to get a lot dirtier than this. So this is nothing new to me."

I went to find some clothes while the bath continued. I figured mine would fit Tony fairly well. By the time we got him out of the tub, dried off, and dressed again, Tony was mumbling a few words of gratitude to us; it seemed as though the warm bath had been the therapy he needed to start the recovery process.

Andy and Cheechee hadn't seen the earlier, pitiful version of Tony, so naturally they were quite curious when they watched us escort Tony from the bathroom and down to the parlor. I discretely took them out on the back porch and explained the situation as I knew it. When we returned to the parlor, Tony spoke.

"Will," he said meekly, as if he were embarrassed to talk in front of everyone. "Now can *we* talk? *Alone?*"

CHAPTER TWENTY-THREE

"ANDY... CHEECHEE," Curtis said. "Let's go down to the Dixie and get some breakfast. We can bring something back for Will and Tony. Okay?" He wasn't asking. He was telling.

I had been Tony's confidant a couple of months ago; I knew he trusted me; that's probably why he was there. In the short time I'd known him, he seemed likeable enough, although I had questioned his close association with Johnny Dempsey.

After Andy, Cheechee, and Curtis had left, I sat on the couch beside Tony. I didn't know what to expect, and I didn't say anything, just waiting for Tony to begin.

"I... I... don't know where to start," he said. His voice was still weak, but sounding more normal now than it had earlier. No more tears streaked his face; it seemed that he had cried out all the anxiety, but I could still sense high levels of fear and emotional confusion.

"Try the beginning," I said. "That always seems to work for me."

Tony looked at me and tried to smile, as if he were grateful for my understanding. "Okay... I'll go back to... well... remember when you hooked me up with Aaron Tyler? The First Mate on the Hercules?"

"Sure," I replied. "I think he wanted to hire both of us that day."

"Yeah... he... I... I saw him again last week... and he... he asked about you..."

Tony was still having difficulty talking comprehensibly, but I thought I should just let him go at his pace until he found a comfort level.

"I told him... I told him that I hadn't talked to you much lately... but that I would... " Tony paused a few moments to gather his thoughts. "He wants you to get in touch with him again... "

"Maybe I will," I said. "Did he hire you?"

Tony nodded, and then he continued. "Yeah... he gave me some papers to fill out... said I could start next week... "

"That's great!" I encouraged.

"But... I'm afraid... it's not going to happen... "

"Why? What's wrong?"

"Well... Johnny and me were hangin' around together again some... and he... well... he was getting back to... his old tricks... following me around... y' know... obsessed, I guess is the right word... well... I thought if I hired on with Aaron on the Hercules... I could get away from him... Johnny... "

"Yes, you could."

"Well... Johnny somehow found out... that... that I would be working on the Hercules... found me at a bar last night... and we drank quite a bit."

My gut reaction was that this is where the story would take a bad turn. Johnny Dempsey and too much alcohol in Tony didn't seem like a good combination. I was still convinced that Johnny could be a bad influence on anyone, but the rest of the Knights of the Square Table seemed to like him well enough to welcome him to every Friday night gathering at the Lion's Den. I knew they were aware of his drug dealing because most of them were his customers. But they probably weren't aware of his warped sexual practices, among other criminal divergences that I had privately discovered from Cheechee and Tony.

"Johnny told me..." Tony continued. "... That he would get

a stateroom... on the Hercules... so that we could still be together all the time."

"So, did you tell Johnny—*again*—that you didn't want to
be with him all the time?"

"I... I tried to... but then he bought a six-pack of beer and
took me out to a lonely spot along the river north of town...
we... we drank some more... and I... I kept pushing him
away... and then I was just going to scare him... I... I had my
back to him and... I had... I had my open pocket knife in my
hand... I didn't realize that he had stepped so close behind
me... and I swung my hand around to scare him with the
knife... and the blade must've went right between his ribs...
stabbed his heart. He fell to the ground... and he never
moved or breathed again." Tony paused and looked into my
shocked eyes. "I killed Johnny," he said calmly. "I stabbed
him with my knife, and now he's dead."

"Are you sure? Are you sure he's dead? Maybe you just
wounded him."

"No, Will... he's dead. I dragged him down the riverbank
and put him in the river. He sank out of sight. He's dead."

I quickly took inventory of all my senses to make certain
that I wasn't dreaming. Now I understood why I had found
Tony in that wretched condition that morning, but I was
stunned by this ghastly account of how it occurred.

"I spent most of the night," Tony went on, "Walking... and
finding my way to the park just up the street. All I could
think of was trying to find you. By then I had sobered up
some, but I was so exhausted and I fell asleep for a while under some trees."

He leaned against the sofa backrest, closed his eyes, and
took a deep breath. "And now I am so tired, Will. I am so
very, very tired."

Exhaustion from re-living that whole scary episode in his
mind again had overcome him. Perhaps some sleep would do

him good, and help him to think more clearly. "You can go up to my room and sleep for a while if you want," I suggested. "You know where it is." I didn't know what else to say.

Tony opened his eyes. "I think I will. But please tell me you'll help me... I don't know what to do."

"Get some sleep, and let me think about it."

"Thanks Will." He slowly navigated up the stairs to my room.

More than two hours later I heard Curtis's Pontiac pull up into the back yard while I sat at the kitchen table nursing a cup of coffee. They didn't waste any time coming in, but they came in quietly. Andy set a paper bag on the table in front of me. "We brought you doughnuts. Eggs and toast would've been soggy and cold by the time we got it here."

"Where's Tony?" Curtis asked.

"He's sleeping up in my room."

"So, did you find out what happened?"

"Yeah, I found out."

"So, are you gonna tell us?"

"All of you," I said. "Sit down. This is serious."

They all sat down around the table, eyes on me as I tore open the bag of doughnuts.

"Did he get into a fight?" Andy asked.

"A rough-ass dance hall, I bet," Cheechee added.

Curtis just sat there patiently waiting for me to swallow my doughnut.

"No, he didn't get into a fight... not like that," I responded.

"Well, what then?"

I took a deep breath, exhaled, and looked each one of my best friends in their eyes. "Tony killed Johnny Dempsey last night."

Just a few seconds passed silently while the statement registered with all of them.

"What?" "Are you serious?" "He killed Johnny?" came

from around the table.

I well expected this to be difficult, one way or another. "Yes, I'm serious," I said.

"Great! We're harboring a murderer—"

"It was an accident!" I said, before the conversation got out of hand. "He only meant to put a scare in Johnny, and he accidently stabbed him. And I believe him. I don't think he's making it up."

I retold the story just as Tony had told it to me. Cheechee fully grasped the concept—he knew Johnny better than the rest of us—and I think Andy and Curtis accepted my logic, too.

"So, what are we gonna do?"

"Other than convincing Tony to go to the police on his own, I don't think we should do anything," I said. "We weren't involved, and I think we should keep it that way."

"We could take him with us on tour... get him out of town," Cheechee suggested.

"No," I insisted. "Then we'd all be fugitives. Better for him, better for all of us if he just turns himself in. It was an accident... he'll get off easy."

CHAPTER TWENTY-FOUR

I WAS beginning to hate this city again. Granted, some wonderful things happened while I had been here: I learned a new skill—photography; I gained some good friends; the city opened my eyes to a bigger world. But now it was starting to show me its mean side, and I was quite sure that I had only witnessed a meager sampling, so far. Uncertain that I could withstand the full impact of any more of its brutal tricks, I thought I was ready to make some changes, and I suspected that Andy, Cheechee, and Curtis were feeling the same way. Since their encounter with that drunken dance hall mob, I'd heard them make mention of a Gaslight Knights "tour" several times but I didn't know if I would be invited to join them. I never asked, and they never volunteered. Right now, though, we stared another serious problem in its ugly face: what to do about Tony.

"We've been talking this over," Curtis said to me. "We've been thinking for quite a while that we'd like to go somewhere else... get out of St. Louis for a while... play in some other towns."

"Where do you want to go?" I asked.

"Don't know for sure. Haven't really decided that."

"And you think now would be a good time to go?"

"Things aren't getting any better here."

"So, you're just gonna take off without a plan of where you're going, and leave me here alone to deal with all this."

Curtis looked at me as if I had lost my mind. "No... you'll go with us... won't you?"

Andy and Cheechee stared at me with expectation. Just moments ago I had felt like I was being abandoned; now, suddenly it seemed like I was being shanghaied.

"But I'm not a Gaslight Knight."

"Sure you are, Will. You're one of us."

I was quite relieved to know they had assumed all along that I would accompany them, wherever they intended to go. I had even talked to Sadie a few days ago about leaving St. Louis, but, of course, then, I didn't have a plan, either. She was just a little disappointed—at first—that I would not be there to help her in the studio, but then she realized that the busy time was nearly over, and she thought it was good that I had decided to explore my horizons.

But before I could leave town, now, I had to resolve my connection to Tony's predicament; I could imagine all sorts of reasons why the police would come snooping. They would eventually find Dempsey's body, and then they would associate him with Tony, and Tony with the rest of us. There were bound to be a lot of questions asked. If I could convince Tony to voluntarily go to the police, though, it might ease the pressure on those who had nothing to do with Dempsey's death. As far as I knew, that included everyone except Tony.

"He should get a good lawyer," Curtis suggested.

"But does he have any money to hire a lawyer?"

"His Aunt Gertrude has money, and she has a lawyer, too."

After Tony had slept another four hours, he seemed to be coherent again, although I could tell that he was still quite suppressed with his situation, and understandably so. At least he could think rationally and had control of all his functions. When I explained to him that I was optimistic about his fate, because Dempsey's death was the result of an accident and not a premeditated act, Tony realized that his chances were pretty good, even though the unavoidable experience with the police might not be the most pleasant.

"Do you know any lawyers?" I asked. "You should really talk to one before you go to the police."

"Yes," Tony replied. "Bob Turner... he handled all the legal custody stuff for Aunt Gertrude when I came here. I got to know him real good."

It was comforting to know that Tony was acquainted with Mr. Turner so well—he addressed him as "Bob" during the telephone call to the lawyer's office. I couldn't hear but one side of the conversation in which Tony expressed his urgent need to see Bob right away. "I'm in some serious trouble, Bob. I have to talk to you right now... No, it can't wait... No, I'd rather talk to you at your office. Can I come right over?"

We shared some late lunch with Tony, and then Curtis drove him away to the lawyer's office somewhere on the west side of town.

I worried about what Tony would say in regards to my connection with the recent chain of events. Curtis and I had given him a bath, clean clothes, and he slept for a few hours in my bed—that's all. But I envisioned that to evolve into providing shelter for a fleeing criminal, or whatever the legal language would call it. And I worried, too, about what would happen to Tony; I didn't think he deserved to spend the rest of his life behind bars. Johnny's death was an accident. I was convinced of that. But then Curtis—good old Curtis—

convinced me that I shouldn't worry. He had known Tony the longest, since Tony started public school. He knew Tony's Aunt Gertrude, and he was familiar with Bob Turner, the attorney. "Aunt Gertrude will pay Bob well," Curtis said. "Bob will see to it that Tony gets fair treatment. None of us were involved, so don't worry."

I tried not to.

A couple of nights later Andy and I heard the news bulletin on the radio while we were waiting for *The Jack Benny Show*. The day before, someone had pulled a body out of the river. It had finally been identified as that of thirty-year-old John Dempsey, resident of North St. Louis. An autopsy revealed he had been fatally stabbed only once. In custody awaiting an arraignment hearing, the suspect, who had turned himself in, admitted to the stabbing, claiming it to be accidental. Police had already initiated an investigation.

"Hear that, Andy? An investigation. Wonder how long it will be before the cops are on *our* doorstep."

"Maybe we should get out of town... before that happens... no matter what it takes."

I thought about that for one, brief moment.

"CURTIS! CHEECHEE! START PACKING!"

CHAPTER TWENTY-FIVE

ПOПE of us had much to pack. To conserve space, Andy and Cheechee managed to get all their clothes in one suitcase, and Curtis and I did the same. A third suitcase accommodated sheet music, notebooks, my camera and film, and other assorted miscellaneous items. All my books and the food in the ice box went to Jesse's house.

"Where are you headed?" Sadie asked. She already knew about our notion to leave St. Louis for a while, and I suppose she thought we had perhaps laid out a route with some sort of destination in mind.

Each of us blurted out a different compass point simultaneously, and then we confessed that we hadn't yet formulated a crystal-clear plan.

"Well," Sadie said. "This time of year, north would seem to be the most logical choice, don't you think?"

We all nodded in agreement.

"How long will you be away?"

"Can't say for sure," I said. "Guess we'll know that when we get there."

"So... you don't know where you're going, how to get there, or how long you'll stay?"

"No."

"Have you planned *anything*? I hope you at least packed some extra clothes."

Now, I thought Sadie was sounding like a mom. "Yes, Sadie. We have *all* our clothes... and everything else we need with us."

"Do you have money? It costs a lot to travel these days, y' know."

"Yes, Sadie. We all have plenty of money to travel."

"And you're going in Curtis's car?"

"Yes, Sadie. It's like new and it's in very good condition... and Curtis is an excellent driver."

"What if you get lost?"

"Sadie... I've been reading river charts for five years. I think I can follow a road map. We won't get lost." I could tell that Sadie had suddenly renewed her concern about us traveling into unknown territory on our own. But in reality, we were all seasoned travelers to some degree. Andy and I had been on the go, up and down the Mississippi River a hundred times, visiting and exploring towns we had never seen before. Cheechee had left Denver on his own, and traveled across the country to St. Louis. Curtis had told us of several vacation trips he made with his parents to many parts of the country. So it wasn't like we'd never left the neighborhood. We were young, adventurous... and we were anxious.

"And where will you stay at night? Hotels? You have to be mighty careful these days of flimflam men and—"

"Sadie!" I interrupted. "We're big boys. We'll be fine."

Sadie finally realized she couldn't talk us out of going. "Andy," she said. "Does your mother know about this yet?"

"I mentioned it last time I visited her," Andy replied. "We'll go there first before we leave."

I wished Jesse had been there; one of his brotherly bear hugs would have done me good right then. But he wouldn't be back in port for two weeks, so I t told Sadie to say good-bye to him for me.

Sadie wished us well. "Write," she said. "At least send post cards... let me know you're okay."

We all assured Sadie that an abundance of post cards would adorn her mailbox. We said our good-byes, and of course, there were four big hugs for little Philip.

With the four of us, three suitcases, a picnic basket, four blankets and a saxophone, the red Pontiac Touring Sedan was northbound, next stop, St. Charles. We couldn't leave without seeing Beth Lorado. She was shooing the last of the "Twinkle, Twinkle" kids out the door when we pulled up in front of the house at the end of Third Street. Beth was happy to see us all, but naturally, we went through the same line of questioning there as we had at Sadie's: "Where are you going?" "North." "How long will you be gone?" "Don't know." ... And so on...

Beth was proud of Andy, and glad that he was spreading his wings. But I could tell that she was concerned, too, for all of us. She had molded Andy into a fine musician, and now he had found his mark. That it had led him to St. Louis, just a few miles away, was one thing, but now, his travels would take him far beyond a half-hour bus ride. It was fortunate that Beth had been conditioned by Andy's being away—albeit a short distance away—for the last several months; that made his leaving now a little less abrupt. But there were still tears, and, of course the last efforts attempting to convince us all to postpone the departure. Even I had difficulty saying good-bye to Beth without shedding a few tears, as I had long ago established an endearing relationship with her when I lived in her house as a boarder, and as her student. She had unleashed that urge within me to read books and to learn. She had taught me so much about the world around me and how to live in it, and I was grateful for that.

"I'll expect letters," Beth said from behind the tears. She was directing the statement to both Andy and me.

"Of course we'll write you." What else could we say?

We hadn't mentioned to Sadie, nor did we tell Beth about Tony, the trouble he was in, or the real reason we decided to leave town at that particular time; it would only add to the concern, and to the list of questions. We just hoped that anything they heard on the radio news broadcasts or read in the newspapers about Johnny Dempsey and Tony Delaware wasn't associated with any of us.

CHAPTER TWENTY-SIX

AND THAT'S how it happened that we left St. Louis. By the time we checked into the Stoddard Hotel we had traveled over 400 miles, experienced—and survived—two flat tires, three million ants, ten thousand bees, a dozen raccoons, two hundred stray cows, a circus convoy, four hay wagons, and one very persistent fellow wanting us to join his carnival troupe. It had been an interesting journey of five days and nights, camping out under the stars mostly, not because we *had* to, but because we *wanted* to. Once we learned how to avoid the ants and bees, and how to combat the raccoons, the rest didn't seem so bad. Aside from the two flat tires, Curtis's Pontiac performed flawlessly. All considered, the trip, so far, had progressed quite enjoyably.

Andy and Curtis called the terrain "mountains" when we reached northeastern Iowa and southern Minnesota; they had never experienced the bluffs and hills of the Upper Mississippi River Valley, and they were quite amazed. But of course, Cheechee had grown up in Denver, accustomed to the towering, massive Rocky Mountains; to him, what he saw in Minnesota and across the river in Wisconsin were just big hills. Nonetheless, they were all impressed with the beauty of the region. Even I was a bit in awe, as it had been several years since our steamboat passed from here, never to return again. A certain anxious excitement simmered inside me as I anticipated the return to La Crosse, where Jesse, Luke and I had spent many weeks in the late summer of 1930. It was there that our steamboating career was born, and where my "new family" started to come together. It was where Spades Morgan (Andy's biological father) made a little magic happen, and it changed our dismal outlook into a prosperous business. (That's when he won the steamboat back in a poker game from the dastardly riverboat gambler, J.D. McDermott. That boat, of course, became the *Madison*. It might not have been magic, but I was only fourteen years old then, so a lot of things seemed magical to me.) Yes, I had some fond memories of La Crosse that were mine alone, and the others would have to experience some "magic" of their own.

Then how, you might ask, did it happen that La Crosse, Wisconsin became our destination? While we were northbound across Missouri, I officially became the navigator with the map in the front seat beside Curtis. Guiding him, keeping our course as close to the Mississippi River as possible, gave us many opportunities for little side trips into the river towns where I had once been, and thought Curtis, Andy and Cheechee would enjoy seeing, too. After all, we were on a trip of discovery, and our only urgency of getting out of St. Louis was already behind us, so we weren't in any hurry.

At a little country store just south of Hannibal, we bought some groceries to complement the contents of our picnic basket, found a secluded spot on a country road near the river and camped there for the night. It was the next day while we were roaming the streets of Hannibal on foot when Andy asked me about some details of my early encounters with Spades Morgan. After I told them the story of when Spades invited me and Jesse and Luke to supper at the Stoddard Hotel, where the plans were laid for the recovery of the lost steamboat, all three—Andy, Cheechee and Curtis—thought they might like to someday see the town where "it all began." During the next three days while we made our way upriver, their interest in La Crosse grew, and because it was the town where I had spent the most time since I left Milwaukee, I was able to answer most of their questions about it. "Just remember," I told them. "That was five years ago, and things are bound to have changed." But a decision was made; La Crosse was our target destination. Whether or not we'd stay for any length of time we could decide after we were there.

CHAPTER TWENTY-SEVEN

FIVE STORIES of brown brick, The *Stoddard Hotel* had seen some interior face-lifting since I last saw it. The new owner and manager, John Elliot, who had taken over the inn several years ago, was in better tune with making a large, luxury hotel more appealing. Many improvements were already completed, and many more were underway. The first thing I noticed was all the new furniture in the lobby, but the renovation went much further than skin-deep. My recollection of that one visit to the *Stoddard* nearly five years earlier left me only vaguely familiar. I remembered it as elegant in 1930, but now it was downright classy.

We took two adjacent rooms on the third floor, 315 and 317, for a week. Andy asked the desk clerk if he knew of a piano anywhere near that he might have access to.

"Why, yes, there's a piano in the Crystal Room," the clerk replied with a mechanical smile.

"Would it be okay if I used it for a little practice?" Andy asked.

"I don't see why not," the clerk said. "Our guests play that piano quite frequently when it isn't being used by an entertainer."

"Great," Andy said. "We'll do a little practicing, then, if it's okay."

"Sure. Mornings are good... there's very few people in the Crystal Room in the morning."

I could see the wheels turning in Andy's head; he winked at Curtis, and I knew immediately that they would be performing some night, sometime soon, in the Crystal Room.

Even though we didn't really need any help with our luggage, a bellboy in his snazzy dark green uniform insisted that he would accompany us to our rooms. He wouldn't take 'no' for an answer as he managed to grasp the three suitcases and one saxophone case, directing us to the elevator at the north end of the lobby. The heels of his shiny black shoes clicked across the marble floor, and then he waited for us with a smile while we caught up to him and boarded the elevator. An older gentleman, the elevator operator, greeted us all. "What floor, Luther?" he asked the bellboy.

"Three," was the reply. "And Carl, you don't have to wait for me to go down. I'll take the stairs."

When we arrived at the two adjacent doors, Luther looked at us questioningly. "Which bags go in which rooms?" he asked.

"Doesn't matter," Curtis said. "We'll sort 'em out later."

"We get a lot of entertainers staying here," Luther said.

His youthful face didn't strike me as one of such wisdom as to determine that Curtis, Andy and Cheechee were entertainers; we had not indicated that fact to anyone here, yet. I threw the bellboy a curious glance.

As if he read my mind, as if the question were clearly printed on my forehead, he replied, "The saxophone… and I overheard you asking about a piano for practice."

I grinned and let out a little chuckle as I dug in my pocket for a tip. "You should be a detective," I said, and then I put the fifty cents in his hand.

"Thank you," he said appreciatively. "My name is Luther. You fellows need anything at all… you just call down to the desk and ask for me."

"We will, Luther," I replied, and then with a big smile on his face Luther turned and headed for the stairs. *Luther is alright* I thought. His friendliness wasn't faked like the desk clerk; it seemed quite genuine and energetic. I liked him already.

It was quite a change for us occupying hotel rooms among all those other people when we had been used to the seclusion and privacy of our house. But the transition from St. Louis to La Crosse had involved lesser accommodations during the last several days and nights, so the sight of comfortable beds was rather inviting.

"Do you miss St. Louis yet?" I asked Curtis while we were getting settled in our room.

"I was afraid that I would," Curtis said. "But I don't… not yet, anyway. Do you?"

I didn't have to think about that. "Not in the least," I replied. "I feel more at home here than I *ever* did in St. Louis."

"In a *hotel?*"

"Well… not in this hotel… but in this town is what I mean."

"How long did you live here?" Curtis asked.

"Jesse and Luke and I were here only for a few weeks, and the only home we knew here, then, was a couple of staterooms aboard the boat that we eventually owned. But I liked the town then."

"It does seem to be a nice town," Curtis said. "I'm anxious to see some more of it."

"Well, I hope you don't expect to find a city like St. Louis out there," I said. "It ain't nothin' like St. Louis."

"What's so different about it?"

"First of all, it's much smaller... ain't no thirty-story sky-scrapers."

"But I saw streetcars," Curtis said. "Town's big enough for streetcars."

"Yeah, and you might even see a traffic jam now and then, too, but it still ain't like St. Louis."

"Well, it doesn't matter," Curtis conceded. "I think I'll still like it. It has a good feel."

"That's what I always thought, too."

"Then, why didn't you ever come back here 'til now?"

"The river," I said. "The Mississippi is a lot friendlier to boats south from St. Louis. Up here there's snags and sand-bars and rapids and shallow water that make navigation more difficult. We didn't have enough experience running a boat on the Upper River... too dangerous... so we just kept running south."

"Oh. I guess that makes sense. So, now that you're here, what d'ya think you'll do?"

"Well, for starters, I'll be your tour guide and show the Gaslight Knights around town. You need to find places to play, don't you?"

"Sure. That's why we left St. Louis... to find new places."

There was a knock on our door. Curtis happened to be closer, so he opened the door to let in Andy and Cheechee.

"How's your room?" I asked.

"Just like this one... it's great," Cheechee said.

"Any good restaurants near?" Andy asked.

I looked at my watch. It was 4:30 and we hadn't eaten since mid morning. "There *was* a place just down the street from here... had a funny name that I can't remember... I think it starts with *B*."

"Well, let's go find the place that starts with *B*. I'm starved."

The *Bodega* was only a couple of blocks away on Fourth Street. Although we were all keyed up after traveling and finally arriving at our planned destination, we decided to postpone any further exploration until the next day. It felt good to sit and relax, eat hamburgers and drink beer, discussing things that were important, and some that were not, just like we had always done at the *Dixie* in St. Louis. Tomorrow we would find post cards to send to those we thought should know of our whereabouts and well-being; and maybe we should write a letter to Leo Majors at the *St. Louis Post Dispatch*, so that he might write back to let us know the outcome of the Tony Delaware situation. There were places to go and things to see and pictures to take, and the Gaslight Knights could begin their quest to determine if Shakespeare was correct in saying that the whole world is a stage.

After a couple of hours, several hamburgers, and a few more beers, we declared that the *Bodega* was our "*Dixie* of the North."

CHAPTER TWENTY-EIGHT

ANDY and Cheechee found another piano early the next morning that the desk clerk obviously had forgotten to mention. In one corner on the second floor was a sumptuous parlor for use by any and all hotel guests and visitors, and adjoining it was a music room. These rooms were large and elegantly furnished, and could have easily accommodated parties with live entertainment. Rich-looking original oil paintings graced the walls, fine carpet covered the floor, and velvet drapes adorned the windows.

"It was actually Luther who told us about it," Andy explained. "The desk clerk prob'ly didn't tell us about it because it's close to a suite that's rented to a permanent resident... didn't want us disturbing him at odd hours."

After we ate breakfast in the hotel dining room, I left Andy, Cheechee and Curtis to their practice session in the Crystal Room and went in search for Luther. He was the only acquaintance I had made, so far, and he seemed like he would willingly help me with a few questions. Though I had spent some time in La Crosse, it was five years ago, and I knew some things would have changed.

The hotel buzzed with activity that morning, people coming and going. Luther was busy helping several people with luggage, and what I gathered from their conversation, they were in a hurry to get to the train depot. But I had all the time in the world, so I found a comfy chair in the lobby and waited until the bellboy was free. When it appeared that the guests seeking the railroad station were safely on their way, and Luther was finally getting a breather, I sauntered over to him near the front entrance. "Excuse me... Luther?" I said.

He immediately turned toward me, acknowledged me with a genuine smile and a unique nod that included a casual two-fingered salute—nothing mechanical or rehearsed. Perhaps he had practiced it a million times, but he had mastered it so well, it looked nothing but natural. "Yes, sir," he said. "What can I do for you, Mr. Madison?"

I was impressed; he remembered my name. I wondered if that, too, was stamped on my forehead, but I finally conceded all the credit to Luther. "First of all," I replied. "You don't have to call me *Mr. Madison*. If I'm gonna call you Luther, then I'd prefer that you call me *Will*."

Luther grinned. "Sure, I'd like that." And then he leaned in closer to me and lowered his voice. "But if Mr. Elliot is anywhere near, please understand that I'll have to call you *Mr. Madison*. That's *his* rule."

"Okay," I said. "I can live with that."

"So, what else can I help you with, *Will*?"

"Well, maybe you can answer a few questions... if you have the time."

"Sure. I'll try."

"Do you, by any chance, know a fellow named Lester Collins? He worked in a bank here in La Crosse about five years ago. When the banks closed, he came to work as the clerk on our riverboat. But I think he came back to La Crosse last fall... said he'd try to get his old job back."

Luther thought a moment. "I was only thirteen years old five years ago... didn't know too many people in banks then. You worked on a riverboat?"

"Me and my brother *owned* one. It burned at the St. Louis harbor last fall. That's why Lester is back here, but I don't know which bank."

"Hmmm. There are several banks in this town, but the name doesn't ring any bells. But I could certainly try to find out for you... maybe someone else here knows him. Your boat burned?"

"Yeah... total loss. The boat tied up next to it caught on fire, and when it was all over, ours and four other boats were destroyed, too."

"Sounds terrible," Luther said sympathetically.

"Yeah, it was quite a shock to all of us."

"So you gave up on the riverboats?"

"My brother and our other partner—he was our pilot— got jobs right away on another boat, a barge tow. But I decided to wait a while."

"And you joined a band."

"Oh! No... I'm not in the band. That's Andy and Curtis and Cheechee... they're the musicians."

"So what do *you* do?"

"I got started in photography... my brother's wife taught me. She has a studio in St. Louis."

"And you're looking for a job here?"

Another of my questions that must have been emblazoned on my forehead; Luther was quite perceptive. "Well, sort of... I guess I wouldn't turn one down. I think we'll be in La Crosse for a while."

"I know a lot of people," Luther said. "I'll ask around for you... Mr. Madison." His gaze fell upon the front desk where a dignified gentleman beside the desk clerk scanned the hotel register. I assumed that he must be John Elliot, the hotel owner.

"Who are those musicians playing in the Crystal Room?" he asked the clerk.

"Hotel guests, Mr. Elliot. I gave them permission to use the piano. Are they disturbing the other guests?"

My heart sank. For the moment I feared that Andy, Curtis and Cheechee were off to a bad start.

"No," replied Mr. Elliot. "They're not bothering anyone. Have you heard them?"

"No, sir, I haven't."

"Well, you should go give a listen."

"Why, sir? Are they that bad?"

"Bad? Heavens! No! They're that good! Are they performing somewhere in town?"

"I don't know, sir. They never said."

"Well, find out what you can... and then let me know." Mr. Elliot strode away, apparently in a hurry to get somewhere. On his way out, he paused and cordially greeted the bellboy. "Good morning, Luther," he said, and then he brushed some lint from Luther's shoulder. "Everything okay this morning?"

"Good morning, Mr. Elliot. Yes, everything is just fine."

"How's your mother? She feeling better?"

"Yes, sir, much better. She just had a touch of flu, but she's much better now."

"That's good. You tell her hello from me, okay?"

"Thank you, sir... I will."

Mr. Elliot acknowledged my presence with a friendly smile and a nod. "Good morning," he said to me, and then he went out the door. As I saw it, he was not only in tune with running a successful hotel; he was very much in tune with his employees, as well. His interaction with Luther didn't appear as just a show for my benefit.

"Mr. Elliot runs a tight ship," Luther said to me. "But he's a really decent man, too."

"I could tell," I said. "But I hope he wasn't upset about Andy and Curtis practicing."

"I don't think so," Luther responded. "I think he liked what he heard, and he probably wants to go where they're performing so he can hear some more. They *are* playing somewhere in town, aren't they? That's why they're here, isn't it?"

"Well, yeah, that's why they're here, but they haven't actually booked any dates yet."

"Oh. You came all the way from St. Louis without—"

"Yeah, it's kind of a long story why we left St. Louis, and I'll be happy to tell you sometime, but for now, do you know any places where they could play?"

Luther pondered a moment. "Well, there's the *Rivoli Theater* across the street... and the *Avalon Ballroom*... yes, there's lots of places in the area."

"That's great," I replied. "They'll be glad to hear that."

Another wave of people checking out of the hotel started gathering in the lobby. Luther excused himself; "I'll see you again later," he said, and then he went to assist an elderly woman with her luggage.

CHAPTER TWENTY-NINE

A DOZEN picture post cards, a new notebook for Cheechee, envelopes, and a box of pencils were in the bag we carried from the *Woolworth's*. It was late enough in the afternoon that we thought hamburgers and beer were in order, and after all, we had to walk right past our *Dixie of the North* to get back to the hotel. We had covered most of the downtown blocks, looking in store windows, and browsing through some. I took pictures of Andy, Curtis and Cheechee in Riverside Park with the big, bronze Spanish-American War cannon behind them. Now it was time to sit down, rest our tired feet, and fill our bellies.

"What should we say in the letter to Leo?" Curtis asked as he took out a pencil and tore a sheet of paper from Cheechee's new notebook.

"Tell him the Gaslight Knights are on tour," Cheechee said.

"And we're having a wonderful time here in Wisconsin," Andy added.

"And then..." I said, "...ask him if he would please write back with any developments on Tony's situation."

By the time Curtis had finished the letter to Leo, he had written a whole page; he obviously had some of his own ideas to include, too. We all signed it at the bottom.

"I have his home address," Curtis said. "I'll send it there instead of the newspaper office. Then we know he'll get it."

While we were all in the letter-writing mood, we scribed messages on a few post cards, too, just as we had promised to do. Sadie and Beth, especially, would certainly enjoy getting four different picture post cards—one from each of us. We figured that would make up for the five-day, four-hundred-mile trip, during which time we sent none. A different desk clerk was on duty when we finally arrived back at the *Stoddard*; he cheerfully dispensed the necessary postage stamps and offered to put our cards and letters in the outgoing mail to be picked up the next morning.

This place made me feel so good; it was as if I had come home after a lengthy visit away. Even though this wasn't my actual hometown, it gave me a feeling of comfort and security, and for that I could not think of any explanation. Other than this is where my new life on the river began. Other than it was a long ways from St. Louis—where the police had probably, by now, knocked on the front door of our empty house several times. I didn't know why I was so concerned about that. Tony's trouble didn't involve any of us, besides him showing up on our doorstep while his trail was cooling off. Yet, it still made me nervous to think the cops would come asking questions and snooping through our house, aware that Tony had been there soon after he killed Johnny.

But there was more to it than that; for quite some time an apprehension was growing somewhere inside me that concerned the lifestyle Andy and I had fallen into. Andy's music career was important to him, not that it was the problem. It was the other activity that surrounded it. Our association with the Knights of the Square Table was where it all started, although some good things came from that as well— Cheechee and Curtis—without them, Andy might not be as far advanced in the entertainment world as he was now. And of course, Leo Majors had made it possible for me to rub elbows with Keith Blake, the *St. Louis Post* reporter/photographer, who had given me some good pointers. But we had been introduced to the temptations the underworld offered, too, and neither Andy nor I could deny partaking of its pleasures. Fortunately, though, we recognized the rough waters we were sailing, and just in time we found a life boat, and paddled back to shore before the ship went down. It was clear to me, now, that the Tony Delaware incident was the catalyst that propelled us away—*our excuse to leave St. Louis*—and we managed to take Curtis and Cheechee with us.

The next morning after breakfast, I settled into the reading room just off to the side of the main lobby. Their library contained one of the old classics I had always intended to read but never did. So I made myself comfortable with *The Count of Monte Cristo* while the other guys practiced in the Crystal Room. I was just getting a vision of the three-mast sailing ship slowly coming into port when a voice speaking my name beckoned me back to reality. "Will? Excuse me. Sorry to interrupt your reading."

I glanced up from the book to find a snazzy green uniform standing there. "Oh! Hi, Luther," I said, glad to see him. "You ain't botherin' me a bit."

"Thought you might like to know... I found out where your Lester Collins works. The night desk clerk knows him."

"Great," I said. "Where?"

"The State Bank, over on Main. It's just a couple of

blocks."

"Thanks, Luther! I'll go over there to see him."

Luther pulled out a pocket watch. "It's only eight o'clock," he said. "Bank doesn't open 'til nine." Then, as if something had jogged his memory he said, "Say, by the way, if you ran a boat on the Mississippi River, did you ever run across an old guy... Augie Bjornson? He had a boat... stayed here when he came to town. I met him when my mom used to work here."

I couldn't believe what Luther had just asked me. "Well, yeah, Luther. I knew Augie quite well. It was *his* boat my brother and I acquired."

"Really? Whatever happened to him? He hasn't been here for years."

"Augie died about three or four years ago," I said. "We buried him in St. Charles, Missouri. That was his home."

Luther's face turned somber. "Oh. I'm sorry to hear that. He was a nice old man."

"He got to be just like a grandfather to me," I said. "He stayed on with us for about a year as our pilot... taught us everything we needed to know."

"He used to tell me sailing stories," Luther said, far-away reminiscence in his tone. "I really liked that old guy."

"Yeah, Augie was special." For just a moment I felt the need to fight back a tear, and then I moved on. Perhaps Luther and I had another mutual acquaintance. "If you knew Augie," I said, "maybe you know another good friend from the river. He used to stay here, too, and he invited me and my brother to dinner here one night... a long time ago."

"What's his name?" Luther asked.

"He's a gambler... goes by Spades Morgan."

Now it was Luther's turn to be amazed. He smiled, almost in disbelief. "Sure, I know Mr. Morgan," he said. "He comes here several times every summer. I haven't yet seen him this year though."

"Last I heard," I replied, "He was headed to New Orleans on the *Goldenrod*."

"Sounds like Mr. Morgan. Then he should be here sometime soon. How do you know him?"

"Well," I said and leaned back in my chair. "Spades Morgan is the only reason me and Jesse became the owners of a riverboat, but that's a long story. D'ya really think he'll be here soon?"

"You can count on it. And I want to hear the story."

"I'll tell you sometime... when you have time. But there's one other thing I should tell you about Spades now."

Luther eyed me curiously. "What's that?"

"Andy? The piano player? Spades Morgan is his dad."

Just then, Cheechee came in carrying his new notebook and pencils. "Hi," he said to me, and then he acknowledged the bellboy. "Hi, Luther."

"Good morning, Mr. Chapman."

Wow, I thought. *Luther is good. He remembers everybody's names.* "Done practicing for today?" I asked Cheechee.

"No... Andy and Curtis are working out some new music, and they don't need me buggin' them right now." He sat down at a reading table and opened the notebook. "I'm gonna catch up on some writing."

"I'll see you gentlemen later," Luther said, and he hustled off to help someone with their luggage.

CHAPTER THIRTY

FOR the second time in one day I got that *"I can't believe it"* look. The last time I had seen Lester Collins was the day he completed all the paperwork for our insurance claim when the Madison burned in St. Louis last year. He took off his wire-rimmed glasses and stepped from behind his desk. "Will Madison!" he said. "What... why..." he stammered as he shook my hand.

"The bellboy at the hotel told me where to find you," I said.

"Is Jesse here, too?" Lester asked.

"No. He and Luke are on one of Continental's barge tows... they're prob'ly somewhere between St. Louis and New Orleans right now."

"And you? What are you doing now?" Lester asked.

I explained to Lester that Sadie had taught me photography and photo developing skills, and that I was trying to be a photographer, but so far, since I left Sadie's studio, I hadn't been working.

"Then, what brings you to La Crosse?" Lester asked.

"Andy has a jazz band now... well, it's just a trio, actually, and I'm traveling with them."

"Andy? Andy Lorado? He's here, too?" How long will you be in La Crosse?"

"If they can find plenty of places to play, we'll prob'ly stay all summer."

"Where are you staying?"

"For now, the Stoddard Hotel," I said. "How 'bout you, Lester? How've you been?"

"Oh, I'm just fine. Got my old job back and everything's just fine. I'll bet you miss that old boat. I sure do."

"Yeah, I do..." Lester and I talked for the better part of an hour reminiscing old times aboard the Madison, and catching up on events since. I told Lester about the mess in St. Louis involving Tony Delaware, that being one of the reasons we came north. I told him, too, about Andy and Curtis opening the show for Benny Goodman last January at the *Arcadia* in St. Louis.

"Benny Goodman! Wow!" Lester exclaimed. "They must be good!"

"They are, Lester. They're *very* good," I said. "St. Louis loved them. Now they just need someplace to get them started here."

"Do they have a name? They *must* have a name."

"They call themselves the Gaslight Knights."

Lester held up one index finger, indicating that he wanted me to wait for something, I did not know what. He returned to his desk and picked up the telephone receiver. A few moments later he spoke: "Mary, this is Lester Collins. Would you please get John Elliot at the Stoddard on the line for me? Thank you."

Apparently, Lester knew a few ins and outs around La

Crosse, including influential people.

"Hello, John? Lester Collins here... Fine, thank you, and you?... Glad to hear it. John, the reason I'm calling, you have some young gentlemen staying at your hotel. Fine musicians. I happen to know one of them personally, Andy Lorado... oh... you've heard them practicing in the Crystal Room?... well, then you know what I'm talking about. Andy was the piano player on a Mississippi riverboat, and his group has been a show opener for Benny Goodman... yes, they *are* available... yes, I'll have their manager get in touch with you... Thank you, John. Good bye." Lester hung up the receiver. "There. Andy has his foot in the door with the owner of the Stoddard... and I'll call the managers of the *Rivoli* and the *Avalon*... and maybe *Carroll's Place* in La Crescent. I know them all."

"But you told him their manager would get in touch. They don't have a manager."

"Will..." Lester said leaning over his desk toward me with a sly smile. "*You* are their manager."

"Me? But I wouldn't know what to say."

"Just tell John that you represent the Gaslight Knights, and that they would like to negotiate for a night of entertainment at the hotel. Then John will ask you some questions, and all you do is answer them... simple."

"What if I don't know the answers?"

"You and Andy have been working and playing together for a long time, Will. I think you know him better than his own mother knows him. Talk it over with him and his music partners first, and all the answers will come. And whatever their regular fee is for a night... double it when you talk to John. Trust me. He pays well for *good* entertainment."

Lester had a way of pumping up my confidence; I was eager to get back to the hotel to talk this over with Andy, Curtis, and Cheechee. I had never mentioned to them about the conversation between the desk clerk and Mr. Elliot I overheard the day before, but now it was a must. I had already experienced a very brief encounter with John Elliot, and I was confident that he was a person I could easily talk to... no different than any of the high-society people that traveled on the Madison.

I almost forgot the real reason for my visit to the bank. "Lester," I said. "I need someplace safe to keep my money."

Lester grinned. "Well, a bank is as safe as it gets," he said.

CHAPTER THIRTY-ONE

JUST a little past noon I flew through the Stoddard Hotel front entrance. Luther was talking to the desk clerk. He saw me coming and met me half-way across the lobby. "Hi, Will. You're looking for Andy, Curtis and Cheechee," he said.

How could he possibly know everything I was going to ask, before I asked? I was definitely going to check my forehead in a mirror first chance I got. There *had* to be something printed on it! "Yeah, I am, Luther," I said. "D'ya know where they are?"

"They said if I saw you, to tell you they were going to the Dixie... said you'd know what I mean."

"Thanks, Luther," I said. "I hafta run right now, but can I talk to you later?"

"Sure... I'll be here 'til six."

The Bodega—our *Dixie* of the North—was moderately busy with noontime diners, but the Knights must have been lucky because they were sitting at our usual table by the window. "Okay," I said as I sat down. "I am your manager now."

They stared at me with weird and wonderful expressions; I wasn't sure if they were merely amused or if they thought I had fallen and bumped my head.

"I just talked to Lester Collins at the bank," I started to explain.

"You talked to Lester?" Andy said, surprised. "He's here?"

"Yeah... he came back to his old job at the bank."

"Who's Lester Collins?" Cheechee asked.

"He was our clerk on the riverboat," Andy explained.

"He handled all the money and the paperwork... and all the legal business for us," I added.

"And I would imagine," Andy said, "that it was Lester who got the insurance payoff for you, too."

"Yes, as a matter of fact," I replied. "He did that, too."

"So," Curtis joined in. "What does all this have to do with you suddenly becoming our manager? I don't mind, but five minutes ago we didn't have one."

"How much do you usually get for playing one night?" I asked Curtis.

"Thirty to forty-five... depending on the place."

"What would you say to *ninety* dollars for *one* night in the Crystal Room?"

"I'd say halleluiah!... manager."

"Ninety dollars!" Cheechee said. "When do we go on?"

"We have to talk to Mr. Elliot," I said. "But from what I heard of the telephone conversation Lester had with him a little while ago, you're as good as in."

"But he doesn't even know who we are," Andy said. "He's never heard us play."

"Yes, he has," I said. "He heard you practicing yesterday morning. I overheard him asking the desk clerk about you."

"When do we talk to Mr. Elliot?" Cheechee asked.

"Just as soon as I can arrange a meeting," I replied. "And I think Luther will help me with that."

Curtis stared at me with an evil eye and a quirky grin. "Does this mean we have to pay you?"

CHAPTER THIRTY-TWO

FEELING so satisfied, knowing that he had helped me lo-
cate Lester Collins, Luther was even more eager to arrange
my meeting with Mr. Elliot. That meeting turned out to be a
lot less formal than I had expected, and with pleasantly surprising results. John Elliot was truly impressed with the
sampling he had heard while the Knights were practicing,
and he liked the advertising opportunity of presenting a
group that had opened the show for Benny Goodman. I laid
out on the table several of my best pictures I took of them
performing on various theater stages and dance halls in St.
Louis. He said he would have *Inland Printing* make some advertising posters, using one of my photographs.

I went back up to my room where I was certain Andy,
Cheechee and Curtis would be waiting. When I entered,
Cheechee sat at the writing desk with pencil applied to notebook; Curtis and Andy sat in armchairs on either side of the
window. All three jumped to their feet. "Well?" they all said

in unison. The little devil sitting on my shoulder told me this would be a good time to have some fun. Without saying a word, I stepped over to the bed closest to them and sat down.

"Well?" Andy said again. "Did you get us the ninety dollars for one night?"

"No," I replied, shaking my head, trying to look serious. I saw how forlorn they all instantly appeared, as if they had been whipped. I almost felt bad for them, their feeling of rejection having such an impact. The little angel sitting on my other shoulder told me I couldn't let it go on.

"I got you one-seventy-five for *two* nights," I said calmly with a straight face.

It seemed like only a second or two had passed when all three pounced on top of me; I thought they were going to break the bed. Obviously, they were delighted.

When they finally eased up on the playful rough-housing, I continued with the full report. "Mr. Elliot is having handbills and posters printed advertising The Gaslight Knights from St. Louis, Missouri performing in the Crystal Room for your dining and dancing pleasure, Friday and Saturday night, June twenty-eighth and twenty-ninth, eight to midnight."

"He's printing posters?" Cheechee said.

"Yeah. He took one of my photos of you on stage in St. Louis... it'll be on the poster, too."

"Twenty-eighth," Curtis said. "That's *two weeks* from tonight. We'd better find a cheaper place to stay."

"Got that covered, too," I said. "If we all move into one room, he'll give us the monthly rate... which is about half of the regular price. And he'll arrange for you to use the music room on the second floor for rehearsals every afternoon if you want... it can be closed off, so it'll be private."

The three of them milled the information around and mumbled amongst themselves for about a minute.

"One other thing," I said.

They all stared at me with question marks in their eyes.

"John told me that if La Crosse likes your music, you can play in the Wisconsin Lounge one or two nights a week, thirty dollars a night... sort of like a house band... but that'll be after the twenty-ninth."

"How much better can it get?" Curtis said cheerfully.

"Does that mean you're going to pay me?" I said with a devilish grin.

CHAPTER THIRTY-THREE

WITHIN a few days a big, colorful, hand-painted poster on an easel sat at the front entrance of the Stoddard; it announced the two-night show of musical entertainment featuring The Gaslight Knights; dinner seating reservations were recommended. A couple of days later, smaller posters started appearing in windows all over town displaying my photo of the Knights on a St. Louis stage, and boasting "the opening act for St. Louis Benny Goodman Show; Dinner reservations recommended; dancing 8:00—midnight, Friday & Saturday, June 28th & 29th." John Elliot was certainly doing a fine job of promoting the upcoming performance. A week before the show, Luther told me that dinner reservations were sold out for both nights, and there had been three requests from other clubs for booking information. They turned out to be the places Lester Collins had mentioned to me; he must've called them like he said he would. Andy, Curtis and Cheechee were already becoming a hot number, and they hadn't even performed one show in La Crosse yet. The only music they had made was behind closed doors during their afternoon practice sessions. Of course, there had been a few curious people listening at that closed door from time to time.

When Curtis saw so many window posters, and then heard of the sell-out crowd, he suggested that they should find a good men's clothing store and get new matching shirts—"Something really nice," he said. Cheechee and Andy fully agreed without hesitation, and off they went. About two hours later, they returned to the hotel room, all smiles, carrying their bundles of new show wardrobe.

Everything was going along just great.

Almost too great, I thought.

I had experienced feelings like that before—like at any moment a wet, muddy dog would run into the room and shake itself dry all over the new carpet. But I didn't want to cause any concern for Andy, Cheechee and Curtis, so I just kept those thoughts to myself and hoped that I was wrong.

Cheechee and Andy had moved into our room because it was a little larger. We had shared our habitat long enough in St. Louis that the closer quarters here did not present any discomfort; there was nothing we needed to hide from each other. But within a couple of days we discovered the necessity to "spread out" once in a while—to flex our muscles in our own space.

I had found a good friend in Luther, the bellboy. Whenever he had time off—evenings, mostly—we would go to the *Bodega*, eat hamburgers, drink beer, and talk for hours on end. It was then that I explained why we called the *Bodega* "*our Dixie of the North.*" Luther said he hoped to travel sometime and see the country, and if he ever made it to St. Louis, he would surely visit the *Dixie Sandwich Shop* at Sixth and Pine.

I told him, too, the story I had promised to tell about how Spades Morgan had saved Augie's riverboat, and how that boat came to be the legal property of Jesse and me. Naturally, one story led to another, and another. The more I told, the more Luther wanted to hear. So I kept telling him stories about life on a riverboat, about St. Charles, St. Louis, the adventures Andy and I had shared... until the *Bodega* waitresses kicked us out at closing time.

Curtis ventured out on his own, too, exploring La Crosse

and the surrounding area in his red Pontiac. He'd tell me about places that even I didn't know. Of course, he had the advantage of reaching farther distances with his car, so he was able to become familiar with a much larger territory than I ever had. He found the *Avalon Ballroom* in La Crosse, and *Carroll's Place* across the river in La Crescent, both clubs having already booked the Gaslight Knights to perform for Saturday night dances. He'd been to North La Crosse, Onalaska, Holmen and West Salem, and found more dance halls and clubs, nearly every one picking a date for the Knights to play. Curtis was definitely not letting this trip go to waste.

Andy and Cheechee frequently wandered over the bridge to the beach on Barron's Island. For as long as I had known him, swimming had always been second nature to Andy, and it seemed Cheechee was rapidly adapting to that as well. Andy had always enjoyed hiking, listening to the "earth's music," as he called all the sounds of nature. Cheechee had been introduced to all of that by his father long ago, too. Their personal interests—far beyond that of performing their music—seemed to just blend together.

We were all content and happy in La Crosse. And so far, no wet, muddy dogs.

CHAPTER THIRTY-FOUR

THURSDAY, June 27th. One day before the Gaslight Knights made their big debut in La Crosse. I'd guess I was more nervous about that appearance than they were. They were good musicians, an excellent combination of talent, well-rehearsed with a repertoire of popular old and new tunes that people loved. I admired their confidence in themselves that kept them in perfect step... and calm.

Late that afternoon the Knights were up in the music room on the second floor for the last practice session before the weekend shows. Once more, I got comfortable in the main lobby reading room with *The Count of Monte Cristo*. Once more, a few pages later, the snazzy green uniform stood beside me.

"Ah-hem," Luther got my attention. "Sorry to bother you."

"It's okay, Luther. Really."

"There's someone here to see you," Luther said.

"Who?" I asked. I expected it to be another club owner wanting to book the Knights for a performance; I had already talked to several.

"Well, he didn't' ask for you in particular, but I know you'll want to see him."

I put the book down on the table and followed Luther to the main lobby.

"Will!" I heard a familiar voice call out. "I'd never guess in a hundred years that I would see y'all here!"

Even though Luther had said Spades Morgan would show up soon, I wasn't expecting such a breathtaking surprise. "Spades!" I blurted out and hastened my step to accept a hug

155

and a handshake. I hadn't seen Spades for nearly a year. He hadn't changed much, but Spades *never* seemed to change or age. The only thing that ever changed was the color of his suit; today it was blue.

"Luther said you'd be here sometime soon," I said. "It's so good to see you... I'm really glad you're here... how long will you stay?"

"Don't know. Never know how long I'll stay in one place. Y'all know that, Will. But I see Andrew and the boys are performing here this weekend." He pointed to the colorful sign just inside the front entrance. "That's quite a surprise...wasn't expecting that, either."

"It was a rather quick decision to leave St. Louis," I explained. "And this is where we decided to go."

"Well, I'm glad you did," Spades said. "Where's Andrew? Is he here now?"

"Yeah, they're up in the parlor on the second floor practicing. Have you heard them play yet?"

"I caught one of their shows in St. Louis this spring... if y'all could call that a *show*. It was at a saloon."

"*That* was one of the reasons they wanted to get out of St. Louis for a while." I went on to explain how the Knights had been accosted in the parking lot at a bar where they had just played. Spades' poker face, as usual, showed no emotion, but I could tell that he was concerned. "But we're here now, and their first big show is tomorrow night in the Crystal Room. "You'll be here, won't you?"

"I couldn't miss something that important," Spades said.

"Oh! But Luther told me both shows are sold out. You might not get a seat for dinner. *I don't even have one.*"

"Don't worry about that, Will." Spades winked. "I know the owner of the hotel... *and* I know someone in the band. I'll get a seat... for both of us. Now, let's go upstairs and pay Andrew a surprise visit." He retrieved something from his pocket and then extended his hand toward Luther. "Thank you, Luther, for bringing me such a pleasant welcoming gift."

I heard the money jingle as it changed hands.

"The pleasure is mine, Mr. Morgan," Luther responded. "I'll take your suitcase up to your room for you."

As Morgan and I strolled to the elevator, he said, "I like Luther. He always takes good care of me when I'm here."

"I like him, too," I said.

Spades had stayed at the *Stoddard* so many times over the years that he knew exactly where to find the second floor parlor and music room. Andy's eyes widened and the piano abruptly stopped producing sound; he sprang up from the bench and quickly met us at the door. Andy had visited his dad recently in St. Charles, but it was still clearly a joyous moment now, too. Curtis and Cheechee knew of Spades, but they had met him only once, just briefly in a dark, noisy barroom in St. Louis. I doubt that they recognized him, and they were somewhat baffled as to the affection Andy displayed toward him.

"I didn't mean to disrupt your rehearsal," Spades said. "I just wanted to let y'all know I'm here."

"You're not disrupting anything," Andy responded. "We do this every day, so it's kind of routine. Will you be here for our show tomorrow night?"

"Sure, I'll be here. It's quite an unexpected surprise that I should find y'all here, so far away from St. Louis."

"Well, Dad," Andy said. "It was Will's idea to come here, and now we have quite a few dates set to play at clubs and dance halls... so we like it here."

"That's good, Andrew. La Crosse is a nice place."

By then, Cheechee and Curtis had joined us at the door, too; they had finally realized Morgan's identity.

"Good to see you again, Mr. Morgan," Cheechee said with his charming smile and a handshake.

"Now I don't remember..." Spades said. "One of y'all is Curtis, and one is Christopher—"

"I'm Christopher; this is Curtis."

"Hello, Mr. Morgan," Curtis said as he offered his hand.

"Boys... I'm looking forward to your show."

"I'll guarantee you, sir," Curtis said, "that this will be a much better performance than you saw in St. Louis."

"I'm sure it will," Spades replied. "That was just a hole-in-the-wall saloon; the *Stoddard Crystal Room* is a pretty high-class place. Now, I'm going to leave y'all to your rehearsal and go up to my room. But I want y'all to join me for supper tonight. My treat. Seven o'clock okay?"

We all nodded our approval.

"Good," Morgan said. "I'll reserve a table. Meet me in the lobby at seven."

Out in the corridor I said to Spades: "I am supposed to meet Luther at the *Bodega* tonight for supper, but I'll see you tomorrow night. I don't want to disappoint Luther."

"Nonsense," Spades replied. "Have Luther join us, too... if that's okay with you."

"Sure, it's okay. I'll ask him."

When Spades and I parted, I immediately went down to the lobby to find Luther.

"You're here to tell me that you can't meet me at the *Bodega* tonight," he said before I could say anything.

How did he know that? I thought.

"*This time*, Luther, you are only *partly* right."

He seemed stunned—but pleased—that Spades had invited him to join us for supper, and I was glad that he accepted the invitation. Luther probably didn't realize, yet, that he had become one of those "very special friends" to Will Madison.

CHAPTER THIRTY-FIVE

LUTHER always wore street clothes when we met at the *Bodega* several times, and that was usually faded blue jeans and a T-shirt, but I had never seen him in anything but his snazzy green bellboy uniform at the *Stoddard*. So he looked quite dapper in a crisp white shirt and pressed black trousers. But when we sat down at the reserved table for six in the dining room, Luther seemed a little uneasy.

"What's wrong?" I asked discretely. "You look nervous."

"I'm not nervous," he replied, glancing around the room. "It's just that I feel a little out of place... I've never been here as a regular customer before."

"Never?"

"Never."

"Well, just relax," I reassured him. "You're with us tonight. You're not at work, and I want you to enjoy every minute."

"Luther," Spades Morgan intervened. "Will y'all be working tomorrow night during the show?"

"No, sir. I get off at six tomorrow."

"Well, then," Spades said. "Would you and your mom like to join Will and me at our table for dinner and fine music?" He looked at me. "Y'all don't mind, do you, Will?"

"Heavens, no, I don't mind," I said. "In fact, I'd like that. Did you get a table reserved for tomorrow night?"

"Of course I got a table. I know the owner... remember?" Then he looked back to Luther. "How 'bout it, Luther?"

"Sure. I'd love to see the show, and I'm sure Mom would,

159

too. I'll see if she wants to come."

"Y'all just tell her that I insist," Spades said.

"I'll tell her," Luther replied. "And I'm sure she'll be happy to see you again. It's been a long time... last year."

I had not yet met Luther's mom, so this meant that I would be sharing a dinner table with a total stranger. But Spades Morgan would not invite an undesirable person to dinner, and after all, this was Luther's mom.

It was good to visit with Spades again after all this time. He filled us in on his recent travels, which amounted to just a little more than the usual riverboat stops up and down the Mississippi. But steamboats carrying passengers on the Mississippi were on a drastic decline. Spades had arrived on the *St. Paul*, but because he would be staying in La Crosse for Andy's weekend show, he wouldn't be aboard when it departed the next morning. Waiting for another boat was nothing new to Spades, and he thought there would be nothing wrong with an extended stay in La Crosse. It was kind of reminiscent of five years ago, although now, we didn't have to make plans for Spades to win back a riverboat in a poker game.

He had all sorts of questions about Jesse and Luke, and about what I had been up to since the Madison fire. He was sad, of course, that the Madison was destroyed, and that another boat had not replaced it. That's where he thought we belonged, on an excursion boat, because our success had been so extraordinary, all things considered. Maybe Spades was right—and perhaps we would all still be together had I effectively convinced Jesse to pool our insurance money to buy another boat. But that didn't happen, so here I was, back in Wisconsin with some new friends, and with a new career lurking somewhere in the shadows.

Throughout the evening I couldn't help but notice that Cheechee associated with Spades so well. Perhaps the reason for it was simply his close relationship with Andy and he was seeking acceptance; or maybe he saw a father figure in Morgan, to fill that void in his life, just like I had done so long ago. But then again, Cheechee's charm was like a magnet to anyone he took a liking to, and he certainly seemed to know how to pick the right people. I was glad, too, that Spades was receptive, and there could be no doubt that he truly liked Cheechee.

"I've written a book," Cheechee told Spades amidst their conversation.

"A book?" Spades replied. "What's it about?"

Cheechee seemed so delighted that Spades displayed an interest. "A boy growing up in Denver, getting into a lot of trouble, and then running away to St. Louis to start a new life." But as he spoke, he gazed at Morgan with a little apprehension; he was not yet accustomed to Spades' poker face that seldom revealed any outward emotions.

"Well," Spades said. "Sounds like it might be about y'all."

Cheechee's face reddened a little. "Yes, sir, it might be."

"I like the idea," Spades said. "What's the title? Where can I get a copy?"

"Oh, it's never been made a book, yet, but I call it... *If I Could Steal the Stars.*"

"Not published? Well, I'd still like to read it anyway."

"I've read it," I said to Spades. I couldn't help myself from butting in. "I've read it, and it's very good. Cheechee is a good singer, but he's a good writer, too."

Cheechee seemed a little embarrassed by my observation. "I have the *only* copy up in our room," he said to Spades. "If you really want to read it..."

"Yes, by all means," Spades responded. "Get it to me tomorrow."

It seemed quite official; Spades had certainly accepted Cheechee. It remained to be seen, though, if he still felt the same way *after* he read *If I Could Steal the Stars*. But I couldn't think of a single reason why he wouldn't.

Luther had relaxed and was entirely at ease by the time we finished our meal. I knew he and Spades had been acquainted for quite some time, but I didn't know to what degree. It became more apparent to me as the evening went on—listening to their occasional conversation—that they were on a more personal level than I had realized. Luther had never let that show in the hotel lobby; there, when it came to the hotel guests, he was all business; but here, among friends, out of his snazzy green bellboy uniform, he could be himself.

It was Curtis who finally exercised good common sense and convinced us all that it was getting late; tomorrow would be a long day.

CHAPTER THIRTY-SIX

THE CRYSTAL ROOM would be a little different from many of the places the Knights had performed: no darkened theater atmosphere; no bright spotlights; no big stage—just a riser where the baby grand sat at one end of the ballroom, a large portion of which was populated with elegant white linen-covered tables. Suspended from the high ceiling by bronze chains, eight fabulous crystal chandeliers cast a comfortable glow evenly through the entire room.

They started serving dinner in the Crystal Room at six o'clock, but by seven-thirty no one was seated except those with eight o'clock reservations. Spades Morgan and I with my *Leica* camera hanging from my neck relaxed in a couple of comfy chairs in the hotel lobby when Luther and his mom arrived about 7:45. By then, there was quite a crowd gathered waiting to be seated in the Crystal Room, so in the congestion we didn't notice their entrance right away. Luther found us, and in no time at all, I understood why Spades had invited them. First of all, I saw an attractive, forty-ish, dark-haired woman, who Spades spontaneously greeted: "Hello, Irene," and then initiated an affectionate embrace.

"Hi, Will," Luther said to me with a grin nearly as big as the lobby. "I'd like you to meet my mom. Mom?"

She turned toward us, still clinging to Morgan's arm.

"Mom, this is Will. Will, this is my mom, Irene."

I offered my hand. "Pleased to meet you, Ma'am."

"And I'm pleased to meet you, Will," she replied. "Luther has talked so much about you."

"I don't know why he would do that," I said jokingly. "I'm not much to talk about."

"Oh, quite the opposite," Irene said. "You and your brother owned a riverboat."

"Yes, ma'am. It was because of that riverboat that me and Mr. Morgan became such good friends."

"Oh, yes, I know," Irene said. "Spades told me all about the night he saved Augie's boat, and now I finally get to meet the young man he saved it for."

"Mom!" Luther said. "You never told me that you knew about that."

"You never asked... and besides, you were too young to be involved with such things as gambling."

"Mom! I was... I was..." Luther thought a moment. "I was thirteen!"

"Exactly," Irene said with a playful smile. "You were *only* thirteen."

Just then, another bellboy in an equally snazzy green uniform—just a smaller, younger version of Luther—approached Spades. "Mr. Morgan?" he said. "I'll be happy to show you to your table now."

"Well, thank you, Richie," Spades said. Apparently he was

on a first name basis with everyone here. "Let's go."

Freckle-faced, red-haired Richie proudly led us to a table just to the left but near the riser with the piano. It looked as if the table had been added, and a few of the other tables had been squeezed together to make ample room. At the center of the table-for-four, beautifully set with silver, linen napkins, and crystal tumblers filled with ice water, sat a little sign that read: "V.I.P.—Morgan."

I looked around at the other tables to see what their little signs revealed; the ones I could see only had names, but no "V.I.P."

When Richie arrived at our table and turned to offer Spades and his guests their chairs, he curiously eyed Luther. "What are you doing here?" he whispered. "This is Mr. Morgan's table."

"I know," Luther said. "He invited me and my mom as his guests."

The redness didn't show so much among Richie's freckles, but I could sense the envy—his co-worker sitting at a table designated for *V.I.P.* But he cheerfully seated us, and went on his way to escort more diners to their tables.

We hadn't more than gotten comfortable when the blonde and brassy Minnie Woods, the very popular head waitress came to our table for our dinner order. A peroxide blonde long before it became fashionable to be one, Minnie was kind-hearted and well-liked by everyone, and she was familiarly known all around La Crosse as "Stoddard Minnie."

"Will, Luther," Spades said. "Order anything you want. This is my treat."

I ordered the roast beef, reminiscent of the dinner with Spades here five years ago. Luther ordered the same. Spades ordered the baked chicken for Irene and himself.

I was still somewhat in awe over the seemingly closeness of Spades and Irene, and then it dawned on me why Luther

and Spades had seemed so closely acquainted the night before. Luther had not mentioned it in all of our conversation.

We were all engaged in small talk about the weather and
the impressive turn-out for the show when an amplified
voice filled the night. "Ladies and gentlemen, distinguished
guests..."

I turned toward the stage to see John Elliott, the hotel
owner at the microphone. I clicked off a picture. The room
fell quiet; John continued. "Welcome to the Stoddard Hotel's
Crystal Room. I hope you are enjoying your stay at the
Stoddard, and your dinner as well. I hand-picked the musical
entertainment you are about to hear... they were the opening
performance for the Benny Goodman show in St. Louis earlier this year... and their music is truly magnificent. So, without further ado, please welcome Andy, Curtis, and Christopher... the *Gaslight Knights!*"

I was prepared to lead off the applause, to ensure there
would be a warm welcome for the Knights, but seventy or
eighty other people beat me to it. I watched as Andy, Curtis
and Cheechee took their places. They had let me see their
new outfits up in the hotel room, and I saw them again when
Luther delivered them back from being pressed, but here, in
this crystal light, their ruffle-fronted sapphire blue shirts and
sharply-creased charcoal gray trousers gave them a striking
air of royalty, the likes of which I had not seen before. I could
tell by the gleam in their eyes and the way they glanced at
each other that they were quite pleased with the friendly
welcome they were receiving, and I couldn't help but think it
would propel them into the greatest performance ever. I
clicked off some more shots with my *Leica*. The applause
hadn't yet stopped when Andy started playing his theme
song, *Happy Days Are Here Again*. Curtis joined in with the
tune, and because this was their usual opening instrumental
only number, Cheechee briskly strolled among the tables,

smiling and shaking hands with whoever offered one. Oh! What a charmer he was! I had never seen them open this way, but everyone loved it.

I'm not entirely sure that the applause had completely stopped by the time Andy and Curtis finished that first piece, and Cheechee came to the microphone. All I remember is the applause rising to a roar.

"Thank you, all," Cheechee said. When the applause finally died down, he continued. "We are the Gaslight Knights from St. Louis, Missouri... but tonight, we are going to make music for La Crosse, Wisconsin!"

More applause continued until Andy began the introduction bars for Cheechee's first song, *I Get a Kick Out of You*. Even after the plates of food started arriving at the tables, everyone took time out from eating to applaud at the end of each song. There could be no doubt; La Crosse had officially put its stamp of approval on the Gaslight Knights.

A couple of hours later, after the busboys had cleared the tables of dishes, and the waitresses were busy taking orders and delivering drinks around the room, the Knights returned to the stage after a short intermission. By then, the applause was more subdued, but still enthusiastic.

Andy addressed the crowd with the microphone this time. He introduced by name his musical partners and then himself. Then he continued: "There's a couple of *very special* people in the audience that I want to give some *very special* thanks."

The room became reasonably quiet; perhaps everyone was curious to see who would get the notable recognition.

"In the audience tonight," Andy said, "Is the man who put me on this earth. My father, Spades Morgan, is right over there." He pointed to our corner table. "I think he came all the way from New Orleans to see the show tonight. Wave to the people, Dad."

Spades rose from his chair, smiled and waved. The crowd clapped their recognition.

"And sitting right beside my dad," Andy went on, "Is one of the best friends I have ever known. He has stayed by me in good times and bad. He helped me launch my musical career aboard his riverboat, and if it wasn't for him, we wouldn't be here tonight. Will Madison ... wave to these fine people."

I was probably the most vivid shade of red that I could possibly imagine, but Andy had just made me feel about as good as I could ever remember, so I didn't care. I stood up and waved to the applauding crowd.

"I should mention, also..." Andy continued as the applause diminished. "... That Will was my very first music partner."

I could almost feel the curiosity bubbling up in the room.

"Will and I played piano duets together for the audiences on the riverboat excursions. They are quite entertaining. Would you like to hear one tonight... *La Crosse?*"

The room erupted instantly in clapping and cheering. It was easy to tell that this was a fun-loving crowd, and they were game for anything.

Andy coaxed me up to the piano, and even though we hadn't done this in a long time, much less, recently rehearsed, we went into our usual routine of me whining about the fact that I don't know how to play the piano, and him trying to convince me that it will be fun. We were already generating laughs and cheers from the audience.

I sat down on the bench, and Andy sat down beside me. I started picking out *Down By the Riverside* with one finger, the only way I knew how. Then Andy began his dreamy version of *April in Paris*. It would've been hard to mess it up—we had played that polyphony a thousand times.

Once again, as it had always done aboard the Madison, we brought the house down.

CHAPTER THIRTY-SEVEN

THE SECOND show on Saturday night was performed before another standing-room-only crowd. Spades and I looked in occasionally, but most of the time we sat in the lobby. Luther was on duty, and it had proved to be a rather busy night for him. The audience included some dignitaries—the Mayor, several city councilmen, and at least one State Representative. The word must've gotten out after Friday night's show, because several reporters and photographers shuffled in and out all evening. I was feeling pretty darn good for the Gaslight Knights.

That night, Spades and I had plenty of time to talk—just the two of us—without interruptions from anyone. By the time the Knights had played a fifteen-minute encore just a little past midnight, we had covered a lot of ground, catching up on the past, mostly, but projecting into the future just a little, too. He asked me several times about what I thought the future held in store for me, and what I planned to do *after this*.

"I guess I don't possess the wisdom—or a crystal ball—to see into the future," I responded.

"Wisdom is achieved to different degrees," Spades said. "And even though y'all don't have that crystal ball you *think* you need to see into your future, you can still make choices that will make the difference between success and failure."

"I still don't get it," I said, a little puzzled. "How can I know I'm making a right choice if I can't predict the future?"

"It's a judgment call, Will."

"Okay, but how—"

"One of the greatest benefits of wisdom," Morgan went on, "is accurate perception... the ability to immediately recognize right from wrong; good from evil; acceptable from unacceptable. It's a matter of understanding your gut feelings, sometimes. You see, most people can easily tell good from bad, but a truly wise person can see that very thin line between good and *best*. And *that* line is what separates a roll of the dice from a sure thing."

I thought about that for a moment. "Like when you won the boat back from Swamp Scum McDermott? You knew that was a *sure thing?*"

"I knew it was the *best thing* to do... the *right thing* to do... for the right people... and yes, I suppose y'all could say I was confident about it being a sure thing."

"But how could you be sure?"

"Will, y'all have to understand that gambling amounts to a psychological game. McDermott didn't realize that I had discovered how he cheats. Knowing that a man cheats at cards is one thing, but when you know *how he cheats*, he is easily defeated."

"So, why did you even bother with us, when you could've rather been building your own wealth?"

"But I *did* build my own wealth that night, Will… wealth that takes time to collect."

I wasn't entirely certain that I knew what Spades meant, exactly. I was still stuck on understanding how to make a judgment call that would let me see the future.

"If one can evaluate and weigh the future consequences of the choices that are available, y'all possess the right wisdom, Will. And sometimes you just have to listen to your heart."

So then I asked Spades what was in store in his future.

"Life on the river has changed, Will," he replied. "At least, *my life* on the river. I've seen it coming for a while, now… fewer boats out there… the kind I rely on, anyway."

"So, what will you do?" I asked.

"Think it's time for me to retire from professional gambling… as I know it. It's time for me to settle into something I can count on, for a few years, at least."

"And… let me guess. You've made a choice…"

"Sure… I've made several choices. Some are a sure thing, and some I'm still sorting out."

"And the sure thing?"

"I've decided to go into business. During my later years of gambling, I found the good sense to stash away some of my winnings now and then. It's become a rather substantial sum, and I've decided to invest it in… a business."

"What kind of business?"

"Well, as much as I'd like to tell y'all about it, Will, it must remain guarded information until I sort out a few details."

I knew Spades Morgan well enough to know that no matter how persistent my inquisitiveness, I would learn no more from him on the subject. Not now, at least. When he was ready, he would tell me.

CHAPTER THIRTY-EIGHT

ANDY, Cheechee and Curtis were all sound asleep. It must've been three A.M. and I was still wide awake thinking about what Spades had said about choices for a successful future. *Sometimes you have to listen to your heart,* he had said, and *learn to recognize the fine line between good and best.* Right then, though, my head was spinning. I could briefly imagine myself staying in La Crosse; Luther had introduced me to the owner of a photography studio who seemed interested in my abilities, limited as they were. Then my mind swooped me away with Andy, Curtis and Cheechee to other parts of the country; and then my heart led me back to the Mississippi and Big Brother Jesse. *Listen to my heart...* Spades said. But Jesse and the river weren't *available* options right now...

I think that's where I finally drifted off to sleep.

Despite the lack of sleep, I was wide awake again by 7:30. I knew the others probably wanted to sleep late—that they would be tired after two long shows—so I dressed quietly and headed down to the dining room for breakfast. It didn't surprise me that Spades Morgan was already there. He waved me over to his table when he noticed me at the door.

"G'mornin' Spades."

"G'mornin' Will."

We chatted over eggs and bacon about the weather, about La Crosse, and of course about the great success of the Gaslight Knights' two shows in the Crystal Room. I could tell that

Spades was quite proud of Andy. It was the first time ever that Andy had been able to publicly acknowledge Spades Morgan as *his father*. I was never sure if Beth and Marion Lorado, Andy's adoptive parents, were aware of Andy's closeness to Morgan; I assumed not, because Andy never spoke of him around them, and I knew Marion's opinion of Spades was quite low. Since Marion had changed careers from the railroad to the river, and since he had eased up on calling me and Jesse "river trash," maybe his attitude toward Spades Morgan might have been altered, too.

"Did you read Cheechee's book yet?" I asked Spades.

"Cheechee?" he replied. "Oh, y'all mean Christopher, don't you?"

I nodded.

"Yes, I did read it... yesterday."

"What d'ya think?"

"I'm impressed."

"With the writing?"

"Yes, it's good... but more with the boy in the story." Spades paused, stared at me. "Is that really his true story?"

"As far as I know, it is.   Before he started singing with Andy and Curtis, we spent a lot of time together when they were practicing and playing shows, and he told me a lot about his life in Denver before he came to St. Louis. Most everything in his book is consistent with what he told me."

"Do y'all think he *really* stole all those cars?"

"Prob'ly... but he didn't do it for financial gain... and y' know what, Spades? Since all of us have been living together under one roof, I've gotten to know him, and I think Cheechee is a pretty darn good guy."

Spades gazed at me with his usual poker face expression. "Andrew sure seems to like him. And he certainly has a lot of talent."

"Yeah... I sure was surprised when he started singing

along with Andy and Curtis while they were practicing, and I was *really* surprised when I read his book. I just hope he finishes it."

"Something tells me he will," Spades said. He looked at the big clock on the wall. "Oh, my! I promised Irene that I would meet her for church this morning... I hope y'all don't mind, Will, but I really must run."

CHAPTER THIRTY-NINE

WHILE the Knights conducted their usual afternoon jam session in the second floor parlor on Monday, I demonstrated my film developing and picture printing skills for John Jacob, the owner of Jacob's Photo Studio. He had a lot more equipment than Sadie had, but much of it was identical or similar to what I was familiar with, so I had no trouble in displaying my worthiness. I guess it was my experience in that specialized field that gave me the edge over several other people who wanted the job. Mr. Jacob seemed delighted that he would not be required to teach someone the procedures of film processing. So within a few days I had settled into a daily routine working at the studio, earning not as much as the Knights were earning, but they were sharing some of their take with me because I had arranged several of their engagements. Fifteen dollars a week, give or take, wasn't quite "riverboat" pay, but at least I was earning my keep.

Andy, Curtis and Cheechee performed a few hours a couple of nights a week in the Wisconsin Lounge, the Stoddard's cocktail bar. When people found out they were there, the place usually filled up. They continued to play at other clubs and dance halls on the weekends, too, so they maintained a rather busy schedule.

I usually spent part of my days off from the studio in the reading room trying to get through *The Count of Monte Cristo*; it was an intriguing story that kept me turning pages. *Edmond Dantès*, the main character had just been imprisoned when I noticed Spades Morgan enter the lobby through the front door; Irene was with him. They paid no attention to my side of the room, but went straight to the elevator where Luther joined them. I didn't hear any of their conversation, but nothing seemed out of the ordinary, so I continued to read after they disappeared behind the elevator door.

A little while later, Cheechee and Curtis came from the upstairs parlor where they had been practicing.

"Luther said you were here," Curtis said.

"I've been here for over an hour," I replied.

"Mr. Morgan and Irene wanted to talk to Andy in private, so we left them in the parlor."

"I saw Luther going up in the elevator with them," I said.

"Yeah, he's in there with 'em, too."

"Is there trouble?"

"They all seemed quite happy, so I don't think there's trouble."

"I wonder what they're talking about."

"Don't know, but I'd bet we'll find out soon enough."

Curtis was absolutely right; we did find out soon, and we didn't have to threaten Andy with throwing him out the second story window to get the answer. Instead, Spades and Irene found us still in the reading room. I knew it must be good news, because Spades was actually smiling just a little. Irene was glowing.

"We have an announcement to make, boys," Spades said. "It wouldn't be fair to y'all for us to keep a secret from you... as long as you know about our private meeting with the other boys. We had to talk to them first... I think you'll understand why." Spades paused, took a deep breath, put an arm around Irene, and then went on. "I have asked Irene to be my wife."

"And I said yes," Irene added with a most joyous smile.

"Of course," Spades continued, "Andrew and Luther needed to be the first to know, and they seem to be quite comfortable with becoming stepbrothers."

A moment later when Spades' announcement registered in my head, a slight breeze might have tipped me over. Curtis and Cheechee rushed over to offer handshakes of congratulations to the couple while I spent a few seconds thinking about what I had just heard. I was indeed happy for them, but I didn't know what to say.

Spades stared at me, as if waiting for my reaction. "Will... say something."

"I... I... I think it's wonderful!" I said.

"When is the wedding?" Curtis asked.

"And where?" Cheechee added.

"Oh, we're just gonna get hitched by a Justice of the Peace," Spades replied. "Nothing fancy... no big wedding, no big parties..."

"When?" I asked as I shook his hand, and then Irene's.

"Twenty-sixth of July... a week from this Friday," Irene replied. "Now, if you boys will excuse me, I must do some shopping in town." She lovingly kissed Spades on the cheek, and then she was off with a song in her heart.

"Is this one of the choices you were sorting out?" I asked Spades.

"Honestly, Will, I have been planning to ask Irene's hand in marriage for over a year. Just been waiting for the right time."

"Is that why you got off the boat here in La Crosse?"

"Will, I never planned to go any farther. I'm not waiting for another northbound boat. The next boat I board will take me and Irene back to St. Louis on a honeymoon cruise."

"What about Luther? Is he going, too?"

"I've talked briefly with Luther," Spades said. "He'll stay here for a while, but then he's coming to join us in St. Louis."

"Oh," I said, and I must have frowned.

"What's the matter, Will?" Spades said.

"Oh… it's just that me and Luther have become such good friends…"

"Will," Spades said. He laid a hand on my shoulder. "Something tells me you'll be coming back to St. Louis soon, too."

"What makes you think that?"

"Let's just say… I know."

CHAPTER FORTY

I HAD BEEN WAITING for the sixteenth of July, but not for any usual reason that most people would wait for a particular date. On the calendar it showed a full moon would appear in the sky on the sixteenth, and I had been watching the waxing moon for several nights. I wanted to try to take pictures of the moon at its fullest, and I had this dramatic picture in my mind with the full moon rising over the *Stoddard Hotel*. It would be great! I had mentioned my plan to Mr. Jacob, and he gave me a few pointers about the camera settings to use, and he loaned me a tripod on which to mount the camera, to make absolutely sure of a steady shot. I already had my spot across the street picked out, where I would be in shadow without any street light casting unwanted brightness on the camera lens, and where I would be in perfect position for a splendid view of the moon just above the roof of the *Stoddard.*

It's going to be a spectacular photograph... I thought.

I didn't work at the studio that day, so I had plenty of time to get ready for the moon pictures that would surely get me recognized as an accomplished photographer. The free day also gave me plenty of time to think about all the other things that were happening all around me, and how my life was apt to change—whether or not I *wanted* it to change.

Sitting alone at the *Bodega* with a cup of coffee as my only companion, I vividly recalled that day aboard the riverboat a few years ago when I gazed into a mirror. I had studied the fellow looking back at me, and realized then that I wasn't a kid anymore, but still somewhat unsure about adulthood, I thought that I would prefer reclaiming my youth and starting over. I knew that wasn't possible, so I accepted my position in the world for what it was worth.

That day, as I reflected on it, seemed a turning point in my life. As I accepted the responsibilities of growing—spiritually as well as physically—I merely stumbled onto the greatest lesson that every person should learn: change the things that need changing; accept the things I can't change; and possess the wisdom to know the difference.

Just a few days ago Spades Morgan had taken that lesson to the next level when he explained to me about wisdom being the ability to recognize *good* from *best.* He was referring to the choices that would change one's life. I understood that concept quite clearly. What *wasn't* clear to me, though, right then, was what my choices really were, for there seemed to be so many uncertainties looming in my future. Spades had even planted a few of them.

Now that Spades and Irene were getting married, it seemed unmistakably certain that they would return to St. Louis, and there didn't seem to be any question about Luther going, too. Whatever "business" Spades was intending to enter probably enticed Luther as well. Perhaps Spades was buying a hotel, and Luther would be the Head Bellboy. At any rate, my friend Luther would be leaving La Crosse...

Although I had not seriously considered my return to St. Louis since the day we left, Spades seemed to think I would. True, my Big Brother Jesse was there, and he had settled in there with his wife and child. To him, St. Louis was home. And because Jesse, Sadie, and Philip were *my family*, too...

What would Andy, Curtis, and Cheechee do in the near future? They had already tasted sweet success in the entertainment world, and by now, they were probably dreaming bigger and better dreams...

What of my career in photography? Had I found the profession that suited me? I still had a lot to learn, but I certainly enjoyed the business, and I savored the anticipation of advancing myself further—perhaps running my own studio someday... somewhere...

Luther wasn't on duty that day either, and he knew right where to find me. I had not seen much of him since the previous day, so I didn't know for sure how he was taking the big news.

"I've suspected for quite some time that it would happen sooner or later," Luther said. "Guess I wasn't expecting it right now, though."

"Are you... ?"

"Happy about it?" Luther finished asking my question. "Yeah, I'm happy for Mom. Spades is a decent man, and I know he cares about her, and I've seen them together enough to know they're right for each other."

"They must've been seeing each other for a long time... your mom knew about Spades winning our boat in a poker game. That was five years ago."

"They'd been spending time together, off and on, long before that... a couple of years, I think."

"What d'ya think about suddenly having a brother?"

"Andy? I like Andy. It'll be a little different not being the *"only child,"* but I think we'll get along just fine."

"So... you're going to St. Louis?" I said.

Luther frowned. "Yeah, and I wanna talk to you about that."

I saw in his eyes a look of doubt, as if he questioned his desire to go to an unfamiliar city. "You look worried," I said. "I thought you wanted to travel... to see the country..."

"Yes, I know I said all that, and I do wanna see the country."

"Then, what's the problem?"

"Well... I've never traveled much. Mom and I went to St. Paul once... on the train... but that was a long time ago. Mom and Spades are going on a boat to St. Louis... their honeymoon cruise, they're calling it. I'm supposed to go later, and I'm hoping you'll come with me."

"I don't know, Luther," I said. "I've got a job here now—"

"Spades gave me *two* fares to St. Louis."

"Two fares? What about Andy?"

"Andy won't leave Cheechee and Curtis... it wouldn't be fair to them. They're a team... you know that."

"Sure, I know that, but—"

"I think Spades meant the second fare to be yours."

I hesitated. I didn't know how I should react. I wanted the choice to be mine, but suddenly it seemed as though someone else was making the decision for me. "I'll have to think about it, Luther," I said.

His face drooped with rejection.

"It's not that I don't want to go with *you*." I said. "It's more like... well... I don't know if there's any reason for me to go back to St. Louis, or actually, if I *really want* to go back to St. Louis. I'll just have to think about it."

CHAPTER FORTY-ONE

IT WAS WELL past midnight when the yellow moon started inching its way over the hills from the east. I was settled into my dark, shadowy spot across the street from the *Stoddard*, *Leica* on the tripod, aimed at the front of the hotel with plenty of sky above it, anxiously awaiting the right moment to start clicking the shutter. The night heat and humidity stuck my clothes to my skin, but I was so excited about my photographs that I didn't really notice the sweltering discomfort. All of La Crosse seemed to be sedated by the heat; not much stirred; only a distant barking dog and an occasional passing car or truck blemished the serenity. It seemed quite unusual.

Despite my anxious anticipation, I couldn't stop thinking about Luther's request. I had all but decided to stay in La Crosse and work for John Jacob for a while, knowing Andy, Cheechee, and Curtis would move on sooner or later. Not that I really wanted to part with their company; they didn't need me as extra baggage, and it was becoming more evident that I wouldn't fit in with their travel plans for much longer. I figured that I would eventually settle into a permanent home, somewhere, and that could always remain as a home base for them, for as long as they needed one. I hadn't mentioned any of this to them, yet, nor did I know their plans, for sure, but it would do no harm to prepare myself for the likely event.

In all its radiance, the moon was slowly approaching the very part of the sky where it would give the most spectacular effect. The stage was set. I double-checked the aim of the camera on the tripod, and made sure the flash bulb was secure. John Jacob had suggested using the flash so the photograph would reveal more detail of the front of the building. "Otherwise," he'd said, "The building will just be a black, square silhouette against a black sky and no one will know that it is even in the picture." It made sense to me, and I wanted to learn, so I had followed his advice.

There would only be a few minutes while the moon was in perfect position, and I wanted to get as many shots as possible, altering the camera settings ever-so-slightly to ensure at least one good picture. I squinted into the viewfinder. I held my breath.

Click. Flash.

Adjust camera. Insert new flash bulb.

Click. Flash.

"What was that?" I heard a voice in the darkness say in a loud whisper.

"Just heat lightning," another voice whispered in reply.

I managed to get about a dozen shots before the moon had slid away in its orbit just enough to diminish the quality of my composition. But I felt confident that the pictures would be as stunning as I had imagined. The next day at the studio I would process the film, and then I'd know.

I shouldered the tripod and camera, and ambled across the street to the hotel entrance. The lobby was deserted except for a bellboy and the night clerk, who were passing the quiet time with a game of five card draw poker at the front registration desk. They were about to hastily dispose of the cards, but when they saw it was only me, they waved with a sigh of relief and continued their game. They both had often seen me come and go with my camera, so they didn't even think to question my late-night activity.

CHAPTER FORTY-TWO

EARLY the next morning, while I was getting ready to go down for breakfast before heading to the studio, there seemed to be more than the usual activity in the hall. By the time I opened the door to leave, Curtis was awake, but Andy and Cheechee were still sound asleep.

"What's all the commotion out there?" Curtis asked, rubbing his eyes.

"Don't know..."

I was met at the door by a bellboy and a blue-uniformed police officer. "Hi, Roger," I said to the bellboy, who I had seen playing cards with Larry, the night clerk just hours earlier.

"This is Will Madison," Roger said to the cop. "He's the one we saw coming in about one-thirty this morning."

"What were you doing out at one-thirty in the morning?" the cop asked.

Taken by surprise, the first thought that came to my mind was that a wet, muddy dog had run into the room. "I... I was... I was out taking pictures."

The officer eyed me suspiciously. "In the middle of the night? In the dark?"

"Yes, sir. Roger saw me come in with my camera." I looked at Roger. Then the cop looked at Roger.

"Yes, sir," Roger said. "He did have his camera on a tripod."

"What were you taking pictures of in the middle of the

night?" the cop asked.

"The full moon," I said. "It was a full moon last night."

"What time did you leave your room to go take pictures of the full moon?" he asked, as if mocking me.

I thought a moment. "I think it was about midnight. Am I in some kinda trouble for taking pictures of the moon?"

"I don't know yet," the officer said. "Did anyone else see you?"

"I don't know… it was rather hot and sticky last night and there weren't many people moving around at that time."

"So you didn't see anyone else… even *in* the hotel?"

"Only Roger and Larry. They were at the front desk when I came in."

"And what are you doing up so early this morning?" the officer asked.

"Breakfast," I said. "And then I'm going to work."

"Where do you work?"

"Jacob's Photography Studio."

The uniformed cop took out a notepad and pencil, scribbled a few notes, and then he said: "I'd like to look around in your room."

"There's three other people sleeping in there," I replied.

"Well, we'll just have to wake them up. I need to talk to them, too."

Curtis was already out of bed getting dressed. He had heard us talking. "What's the problem?" he said.

"ANDY! CHEECHEE!" I called out. "Get up. A policeman wants to talk to you."

They both sat up in bed, yawning and stretching. The cop stepped into the room, immediately examining all corners, behind the chairs, in the bathroom, and then he knelt down and peered under both beds. He stopped a moment when he discovered my camera still mounted on the tripod, scribbled some more notes, and then he stepped to the foot of the bed and faced Andy and Cheechee. Curtis was standing beside them, too.

He started to ask their names, but stopped short. "Hey," he said. "You're those musicians I saw at…" He cut himself short again.

"Yes, sir, we prob'ly are," Andy said. "Why are you in our room?"

"Just want to ask you a few questions, if you don't mind."

"What about?"

"About what you were doing last night."

"When last night?"

"All night."

"Well, after our practice, we went to the Dixie—I mean the *Bodega*—for supper. We met Will and Luther there."

The cop glanced at me.

I nodded.

"Then what did you do?" he asked.

"We went to see a movie at the *Rivoli*."

"What movie was playing?"

"Alfred Hitchcock… *The Thirty-nine Steps.*"

"Where do you practice?"

"In the music room next to the parlor on the second floor."

The cop's eyebrows raised. "What time did you leave there?"

"About five."

"Did you notice anything unusual in the parlor then?"

"What d'ya mean… unusual?"

"Did you see anything missing?"

Andy looked at Cheechee and then Curtis. They all seemed quite puzzled. "No… not that I know of… what's missing?"

The cop sighed a deep breath. "There are three very expensive paintings missing from the parlor."

"Well, they weren't missing at five. I would've noticed,"

Andy said.

"What did you do after the movie?"

"We came back here and went to bed."

"What time?"

"I think it was about eleven-thirty."

"Did you use the elevator or the stairs?"

"Elevator."

"So you weren't on the second floor at all at eleven-thirty?"

"No sir."

"Did you see anyone else in the hotel when you came in?"

"Just the night clerk... Larry. If someone carried those paintings out of the hotel, Larry and Roger are the ones who would have seen them do it."

"Well, they didn't," the cop said. "And so I think the paintings never left the building." He stepped to the door. "Thank you, gentlemen. Sorry to bother you." And then he left.

I think he was satisfied that none of us had taken the paintings, but something told me we hadn't seen the last of him.

CHAPTER FORTY-THREE

THE DELAY with the police officer had cut my breakfast time short, and I was still five minutes late getting to the studio. Mr. Jacob understood, though, when I explained the situation.

"Who would be bold enough to steal paintings from a hotel?" he asked. "And how could they get them out without someone seeing?"

"I don't know," I replied. "And neither do the police."

It was mid-afternoon when I had finished all my work. I told Mr. Jacob that I was off the clock, and that I wanted to stay a while longer to process my film of the moon pictures.

"Take all the time you want," he said. "I'm curious to see how they turned out, too."

Developing film had become one of those "second nature" tasks to me, so all day my thoughts had been bouncing back to Luther and *the extra fare to St. Louis*. I liked my job with Mr. Jacob, and he seemed quite willing to let me advance; there was little doubt in my mind that I would be shooting portrait photographs in his studio sometime in the future.

But Luther seemed so desperate. Then I recalled the comment from Spades; he seemed certain that I would return to St. Louis. He must've known something that I didn't.

All of my pictures developed quite nicely. I was a little disappointed that the moon wasn't nearly as spectacular as I had anticipated; it was merely a large white spot just above the roofline of the hotel. But the Stoddard was identifiable with much more detail than I had expected from a nighttime shot.

I printed most of the frames five by seven inches, but a couple of the ones I thought were the best I printed eight by ten. As I hung the finished photos on the drying clips I took a little time to admire my work. It was then that I noticed something in one of the eight by tens; there was something more in my pictures that I hadn't counted on.

"Mr. Jacob!" I called out to the studio owner. "Come and look at these photos."

While he studied the pictures, I pointed out the extra feature that I had noticed. "Oh my," he said. "I think you've accidentally solved a mystery."

The prints weren't dry yet, but I had to get back to the hotel immediately. "I'll come back for these later when they're dry," I said. I think Mr. Jacob understood the reason for my hasty exit when I took off my apron and tossed it aside. I ran the six blocks to the hotel. Luther met me in the lobby.

"You ran all the way here from work," he said.

This time it was quite obvious how he knew; I was sweating and nearly out of breath so I could hardly speak. "Yes... you're absolutely... right... can you... find... Mr. Elliott? I... need to see him... right away!"

"It's about the missing paintings, isn't it?" Luther quizzed.

I nodded. *Good guess*, I thought.

Luther grabbed my arm and guided me to the elevator where the operator stood at the open door. "Second floor, Carl," he said as he whisked me into the elevator car. "Mr. Elliott is up in the parlor with a detective and you're too out of breath for the stairs right now."

"Oh... you noticed... thank you."

Luther laughed as Carl shuttled us upward, and then he walked me slowly from the elevator to the parlor so that I might catch my breath. John Elliott stood with his arms folded across his chest, staring at a blank space on the parlor wall; another man dressed in a gray suit—the detective, I assumed—stood beside him.

"That was one of my favorite *Monet* originals," Mr. Elliott said. "I paid over a thousand dollars for it…"

Not so strange that I should know the painting that John was imagining on the empty wall, for I had examined all those paintings and admired them many times. I recalled a flowered patio setting overlooking an ocean harbor with sailboats and steamships. *A thousand dollars!* I thought. *No wonder why everyone was concerned about its disappearance.*

The gray-suited man noticed Luther in the open doorway; he nudged Mr. Elliott and pointed to the bellboy.

"Yes, Luther," John said. "Do you need me for something?"

"Excuse me, sir," Luther said. "One of our permanent residents would like to talk to you about the missing paintings."

"Who?"

"Mr. Madison, sir." He stepped aside to allow me through the door.

By then I had regained normal breathing, but I was still quite excited with my discovery. "Did you find the paintings yet?" I said.

"Why, no… we've searched every room, but the police seem to think—"

"I know how they left the building!" I interrupted.

Immediately the gray-suit was inches from me. "I'm Sam Anderson, Police Detective," the man said. "How do you know that?" he asked.

"I was out taking pictures of the full moon last night," I began to explain.

"Oh… so you're the young photographer the officer questioned this morning."

"Yes, sir, Mr. Anderson. You need to see my photos. They lowered the paintings with a rope from a second story window on the alley side of the building... where it's dark and no one saw them. It shows up quite clear in my pictures."

There was renewed excitement in both John Elliott and Detective Anderson. "Where are the pictures?"

"They're still drying at the studio where I work. I just developed them a little while ago."

"Well, let's go have a look."

Detective Anderson drove me and John Elliott to Jacob's Studio in his car. The hotel owner was extremely encouraged, but Anderson warned him: "This doesn't mean we found the paintings, John. It only means we know they're not in the building anymore."

When we arrived at the studio, Mr. Jacob was studying one of my photos. "Ah, Detective Anderson," he said. "I figured you'd be here soon."

CHAPTER FORTY-FOUR

FOR THE FOURTH TIME in my young life, I had aid-ed the police in rounding up dangerous criminals. The first was in Alma, Wisconsin, right after Jesse rescued me from the flood. A scoundrel drifter tried to kill Jesse and steal his val-uables, but I beaned him with a rock before he could do the nasty deed. The police found him deliriously wandering about the next day. Turned out he was wanted in several states. The second was in Northern Wisconsin when Jesse and I tangled with a couple of crooks who robbed several country general stores and stole a car. The third was when me and Andy, Luke and some other deckhands captured a pair of river pirates in the coal bin aboard the Madison down in Cape Girardeau, Missouri. All those times, I guess my life had been in danger, threatened with weapons by violent out-laws. I don't know how *dangerous* thieves of fine art can be, and considering all I did this time was take a few pictures, I can't say that I was threatened or in danger... that I am aware of, that is.

What I can say, though, is that my photography skills be-came rather well-known in La Crosse. John Elliott used my pictures to determine which room the man was leaning out of the window. The hotel guest register identified who occu-pied that room, and after the police tracked him down—and his accomplice—and recovered the stolen paintings, my pic-torial account of the act (four photos that revealed one man in the second story window, his accomplice in the dark alley below, and the paintings suspended by a rope between them) appeared on the front page of the *La Crosse Tribune* along with a story about how I happened to capture the criminal act on film. You might say that I had taken the first step in becoming a photo journalist, but I doubt that the *La Crosse Tribune* was considering my employment just yet.

Friday July 26th was a day of mixed emotions for me; Edward "Spades" Morgan and Irene Holt were married at their private little ceremony that lasted only ten minutes in Irene's house on Market Street. Only Andy, Luther, Curtis, Cheechee, me, and a couple of Irene's closest friends were there. Because it was the middle of the afternoon, John Elliott gave Irene the use of the Crystal Room for a private dinner party, and he insisted that he would provide all the food and service—said it was his wedding gift to her, a friend and former employee of the hotel, and Spades, a long-loyal patron. The Crystal Room was about twenty times larger than was necessary for ten people, but the piano was there; Andy provided a pleasant musical atmosphere while we all enjoyed a few drinks and conversation after the dinner. It was a most joyous occasion.

For me, that day also meant a time when the departure of my good friend Luther was drawing near. Spades and Irene already had passage booked; they would check into their stateroom on the steamer *St. Paul* the next morning, and they would arrive at St. Louis in about four days. Luther's plan was to leave in about two or three weeks. It seemed odd that Spades had not mentioned to me anything more about my return to St. Louis... that he had been so sure of happening. Maybe he had changed his mind.

Andy, Cheechee and Curtis were playing a show that night at the hotel in Trempealeau, a small town about twenty miles upriver from La Crosse. The *Trempealeau Hotel* was a popular weekend night spot, and the Knights' growing popularity assured a full house. I hadn't been to any of their shows for a while, and neither had Luther, so I convinced him that we should go.

"How will we get there?" Luther asked.

"I checked the train schedule this morning," I replied. "There's a train to Trempealeau at eight p.m., and one that returns to La Crosse at midnight."

"Why don't we just go in the car with Curtis?"

"Because they're staying there overnight, and your mom and Spades are going, too."

CHAPTER FORTY-FIVE

SATURDAY was a day off for me, so there would be no need to get up early; I wasn't concerned about being out late. It would also afford me plenty of time for a farewell visit with Spades and Irene before they sailed off to St. Louis—Andy was saying his good-byes now, because he and Curtis and Cheechee would be staying in Trempealeau for another show Saturday night.

Right after our celebration dinner party broke up I went to the train depot to buy all the tickets so Spades couldn't. I knew he'd try to pay for everything again, like he usually did. I always appreciated his generosity, and he knew it. But this time, it was going to be *my* treat.

Spades, Irene, and Luther met me in the hotel lobby about seven-thirty; we walked to the train depot, and just as I suspected he would, Spades pulled out his wallet. I held up my hand to stop him, and then passed around the tickets. "My treat," I said with a big smile. "You didn't want any wedding gifts, so consider tonight a going-away party... on me."

"Will," Spades said. "That's mighty thoughtful of you."

We rode the train for about thirty minutes, and then it was a five minute walk to the *Trempealeau Hotel*. The Gaslight Knights were advertised on a sign at the entrance. They hadn't started playing yet, but when we found one of the last vacant tables at the perimeter of the dance floor, they were just getting ready. Their ruffled blue shirts—the ones they wore for their first show in the Crystal Room—glistened under the lights and Curtis's saxophone sparkled more than his new red Pontiac on a sunny day.

The crowded room broke out in cheers and whistles when Andy began his theme song. Curtis soon joined in, and there was Cheechee shuffling around among the people, smiling, shaking hands, pouring on the charm, just like he had done at that first show. This was *their* style, and the audience loved it.

The Knights had performed three or four numbers when a young gentleman sitting at the next table leaned over between me and Spades. "These guys are great, aren't they?"

I nodded and grinned.

Spades calmly said, "Well, of course they are. The piano player is my son."

The young man gave a pleasantly surprised smile. "Well, then you must be Mr. Morgan. Andy and I were talking at the bar a while ago... he said you got married today."

"I did indeed," Spades replied. He put his arm across Irene's shoulders. "And this is my lovely bride, Irene."

"Pleased to meet you both. I'm Fischer Blinn," he said as he offered his right hand. "I'm the resident engineer at the Trempealeau dam project."

Spades shook his hand, and then introduced Luther as his new stepson, and me, his "long-time riverboat friend."

Fischer threw me a puzzled stare.

"Me and my brother," I explained, "owned an excursion boat on the Mississippi. Mr. Morgan helped us acquire it in La Crosse a few years ago."

"Where's your homeport? La Crosse?" Fischer asked.

"St. Charles for a couple of years, and then St. Louis. We didn't have the experience to run the Upper Mississippi."

"The dams and locks we're building now will make it a better river to navigate."

"Yeah, I know. I've been reading about them."

"Where's your boat now?"

"Oh, the Madison burned at St. Louis last year."

"Sorry to hear that," Fischer said frowning. "So you're just here visiting?"

"I'm here with the band. Andy's my best friend. He was the entertainment on the Madison."

Fischer fit all the pieces together quite easily, and because we had a common interest—navigation on the Mississippi River—we talked a lot. He explained how the locks would work once they were operational, and how the dams controlled the water depth, making navigation for bigger boats possible. I told him of my experiences on the river, and about Jesse and Luke piloting barge tows on the Lower Mississippi. We had so much to talk about that the night slipped by rather quickly for me.

About eleven o'clock, Spades pointed to his open pocket watch. "I hate to cut this short," he said. "But we have to get to the depot."

I acknowledged, and then I said to Fischer, "I live at the *Stoddard Hotel* in La Crosse now. I go to the *Bodega* for supper a lot. Stop in and see me sometime."

"Sure, I will," Fischer replied. "My good friend Francis Landrieu lives on Market Street. I go to La Crosse to see him often. In fact, Francis told me about the Gaslight Knights... he saw them at the *Avalon Ballroom* a couple of weeks ago."

"Well, next time you're in town, look me up."

CHAPTER FORTY-SIX

TWO HOURS after the *St. Paul* had steamed southbound out of La Crosse harbor with Spades and Irene aboard, Luther found me in the reading room with *The Count of Monte Cristo* laid open in front of me, but I wasn't focused much on reading that day. Luther had traded his Friday afternoon work hours for another bellboy's Saturday morning. It was a little past noon; he was off for the rest of the day, had already changed into a T-shirt and jeans, and he was hungry.

"Wanna go to the Dixie?" he said. "You're not concentrating on *Edmond Dantes*, so let's go eat."

"You've read *The Count of Monte Cristo?*"

"Yeah... about a year ago. It's a little hard to follow sometimes, but otherwise it's pretty good."

I couldn't disagree; at times I found myself confused with all the French names and keeping track of who they were, but how did Luther know my mind had wandered away from the book?

"So... are you interested in food?" he asked.

I closed the book. "Sure. I'm starved."

"Did you see them off this morning?" Luther asked while we walked to our favorite cafe.

"Yeah... I had a nice visit with them. They seemed very happy."

"Mom's been head-over-heels with Spades since the day she met him."

"Luther... I don't mean to be nosey, but what about your

real father?"

"My father was killed in the World War. Mom was pregnant with me when he left for Europe, so I never knew him."

Luther didn't seem distraught about his real father, but I guessed there was a logical explanation: how could he miss someone he never knew? But he did appear to be quite content with his mother's marriage to Spades. He'd known Spades for longer than I had, and I wondered if I would ever hear him address Spades as "Dad."

With the noon-hour rush, the *Bodega* was crowded; our usual table by the window was occupied, so we found another in the far corner. When our waitress finally came to take our order, she apologized for the delay. "We've been really busy today."

"That's okay, Susan," I said smiling. "We're suffering from severe hunger pains and I'm sure we'll pass out any minute... but we've got plenty of time for recovery."

Susan laughed. "Yes, you *are* looking rather pale."

"So, could we get a couple orders of your roast beef special? Y'know... to prevent our premature demise?"

"Sure... mashed potatoes and gravy?"

"Yup... and a *Coke* for me."

"I'll have the same," Luther said.

A very short time later, Susan returned with our food and drinks. There was advantage in being a regular customer.

"Luther," I said as I dug into the mashed potatoes. "Has Spades told you about the business he's starting?"

He looked at me with surprise. "I... I'm sworn to secrecy," he said.

"So he *has* told you about it."

Luther only nodded and bit into his roast beef.

"What kind of business is it?"

"Can't tell you... I'm sworn to secrecy."

"Is that why you're going to St. Louis?"

Luther just smiled and chewed.

"Are you gonna work for him?"

Luther smiled some more and shrugged his shoulders.

"He's buying a hotel, isn't he?" I asked.

Luther smiled, swallowed, took a sip of his Coke.

"Come on, Luth… you can tell me. Is it a hotel?"

"There are some things he has to work out yet, and in the meantime… I'm sworn—"

"I know," I interrupted. *"You're sworn to secrecy."*

Quite obviously I wasn't going to get the answer I wanted from Luther, but his reaction to my line of questioning led me to believe that I was correct about the hotel. For any more than that, I would just have to wait.

"Have you thought about coming with me to St. Louis?" Luther asked.

"Yeah, I've thought about it," I said. "But I still haven't come up with any good reasons to go back there, and I like my job at Jacob's Studio. Unless Andy and Curtis and Cheechee decide they want to go back, I'll prob'ly stay here."

CHAPTER FORTY-SEVEN

IT WAS NEARLY four o'clock Sunday morning when Andy, Cheechee and Curtis came back from Trempealeau. I woke up as soon as the door opened, but they must've been so tired that they barely said a word between them, and within seconds, it seemed, they were undressed, in bed and sleeping.

They finally woke up about noon and when I was nowhere in the hotel, they came to the *Bodega* for some lunch. I had been there a while waiting for Luther.

"Thought we'd find you here," Andy said. They made themselves comfortable around our usual table by the window.

"I'm waiting for Luther," I said. "Didn't want to wake you. Why did you get home so late? It was four o'clock."

"We met a man at the *Trempealeau Hotel* last night, and he wanted to talk to us after the show."

"What did he want to talk about?"

"Will..." Andy said. I sensed a little reluctance in his hesitation. "I know you love your job at the studio."

I nodded. "Yeah, I do."

"And I know you like this town."

I nodded again.

"But what would you say if I told you we have *big* opportunities waiting for us elsewhere?"

You see? I told myself. *You knew this was coming.* "What do you mean?" I asked as if I had not given it a thought.

"Thomas Conrad, the guy we met last night, is an entertainment agent. He was passing through here on his way from Minneapolis. Somehow he heard about us and he showed up at the *Trempealeau Hotel* to see our show."

"So, is he *your* agent now?"

"No... we didn't make any deals or promises."

"But he wants you to come to Minneapolis."

"No..." Andy looked at Curtis and Cheechee for help.

Curtis answered. "Mr. Conrad wants us to come to New York."

"You see," Cheechee chimed in. "Conrad is to New York like Harry is to St. Louis."

"Oh," I replied. "Like the Harry that left you hanging out to dry after about a dozen shows."

"This will be different," Andy said.

"How?"

Curtis cut in again. "New York is bigger—much bigger—a hot spot for entertainers..."

"And recording studios," Cheechee added.

"Do you trust this Mr. Conrad?"

"He seems like a straight-up guy," Curtis replied. "But like Andy said... we didn't make any deals. We told him we'd think about it... and that we'd contact him if we decide to go there."

"Have you thought about it?" I asked.

"We have two more weekends to play here," Andy said. "We'll make our decision by then."

"What about you, Will?" Cheechee said. "Are you going with us... if we go?"

I felt a lump in my throat. "I... I... I love you guys like brothers... I think you know that."

They all nodded.

"And you know that I'd prob'ly do anything to help you."

They all nodded again.

"But I'd just be extra baggage for you, and what would a

guy like me do in New York? I hate big cities... *remember*? If you go, I think you'll be going without Will Madison."

"So, what will you do if we go?" Andy asked.

"Oh, I think I'll stay here in La Crosse for a while... keep working for Mr. Jacob... get a house... one you guys can come back to anytime you want."

"So..." Andy said. "Are you saying that you approve of us going to New York?"

"Do you *need* my approval?"

"As our best friend... yes."

"Well then, I guess you have it."

CHAPTER FORTY-EIGHT

AT ABOUT ten o'clock Tuesday morning there was a knock on our door. Cheechee and Andy had left for a late morning swim; Curtis and I relaxed in the room after an early morning hike on Grandad's Bluff. We certainly weren't expecting company, and Andy or Cheechee wouldn't be knocking. I opened the door to see Luther's snazzy green uniform.

"G'mornin' Luther. C'mon in."

"Oh, I can't stay," he said. "I just brought this letter that came in the mail for Mr. Curtis Owens. It was addressed to the wrong room number. I wanted to make sure he got it."

"Well, thank you, Luther," Curtis said as he stepped over to the door.

Luther handed him the envelope. "I'll see you later," he said to me. "Tonight at the Dixie?"

"Tonight at the Dixie," I replied. "Seven o'clock."

"It's from Leo in St. Louis," Curtis said as I closed the door.

It had slipped my mind that we had written to Leo just after we arrived in La Crosse; I hadn't been thinking much about the Tony Delaware/Johnny Dempsey incident lately, but suddenly there was a spark of renewed interest. I patiently waited for Curtis to open and read the letter. "So, what does he have to say?" I asked.

"Well," Curtis said. "It's not terrifically good news, but I guess it's kinda what we expected."

"About Tony?"

"Yeah. Leo says that the Knights of the Square Table have dispersed: "With the four of you in Wisconsin," he read from the letter, "Marty and Milo gone back to New York, Johnny dead and Tony in jail, it's only me and Frank that show up at the Lion's Den on Friday nights."

"Marty went back to New York?"

"Sounds like it," Curtis replied, and read aloud some more of Leo's letter: "A week after Milo came back from college, they both left to go back to New York City."

"Hmmm. Marty must've gotten homesick," I said. "So Tony is in jail?"

Curtis continued to read aloud from the letter: "Court proceedings moved swiftly. Johnny's death was ruled accidental, and considering that Tony was acting in self-defense, he might have gone free without any jail time if he had not dumped the body in the river and had gone to the police right away that night. Even the fact that he had been drinking quite heavily and perhaps not thinking clearly did not sway the court's decision from a one-year prison sentence."

"Poor Tony," I sighed.

"You should be saying *lucky Tony*," Curtis replied. "Only one year... I'd say he got away with murder."

"But it was an accident," I protested.

"Think about it, Will. Why did he dump the body in the river if it was an accident? I'll go along with the self-defense idea... maybe... but I'm not so sure about the accidental part."

Maybe Curtis was right. Maybe I had been seeing only the black and white of the issue. Tony seemed to be a good fellow, but maybe I had trusted his word a little too far.

When Andy and Cheechee came back from the beach, Curtis read the letter to them, too. Their reaction was less sympathetic toward Tony than mine had been; time had obviously diluted their concern. But we all agreed that even though Tony was our friend, we had done the right thing by avoiding any involvement; leaving St. Louis had been our best option.

Little did it matter now. In all the letters I had received from Sadie during the summer, never once did she mention that the St. Louis Police came looking for me.

CHAPTER FORTY-NINE

I SAT at our regular table by the window at the *Bodega*, but I was alone—very alone. Me and the Knights had spent quite a summer in Wisconsin. They had taken their music career to another plateau, and now it seemed they would soon be off on an adventure that could take them around the world, perhaps. They had only one more scheduled engagement here, and there was little doubt in my mind that they would leave for New York soon after. It was all they had been talking about lately.

I reminded myself that it was Wednesday August 7th; one week from today, Luther would board the steamer *St. Paul*, bound for St. Louis, and I wondered if I would ever see him again. I wondered if I would ever see the Knights again. This separation could very well be the end of an era that I would not soon forget.

Even though all my closest friends were leaving soon, I felt good about my job with Mr. Jacob; *my* new career was off to a good start, too. A sense of security washed over me. I thought about the uncertainty I would face if I went with Andy and the boys to New York, and St. Louis was just that big city that I didn't much care for. Here, I had a good job, I had money in the bank, and I could still be close to the river that I loved. All things considered, I had justified my staying in La Crosse.

Right in the middle of my revelations, I noticed someone standing next to the table. "Hi, Will. Remember me?" he said.

I gazed up at the face; it was familiar, but it took me a few seconds to associate it with a name. "Oh! Hi, Fischer!" I said when I recalled our meeting at the *Trempealeau Hotel*. "Have a seat. I'm here alone."

"Thank you," Fischer said as he sat down. "I came to La Crosse to see my friend, Francis, and I thought I'd look you up, too."

"Well, I appreciate that," I replied.

"You weren't at the *Stoddard*, and I remembered you saying that you came here a lot."

"Yeah, this is my favorite place to eat... or to drink coffee... or to just think."

"I see you must be here drinking coffee tonight."

"And thinking."

"Oh... did I disturb you?"

"No, not at all. I'm glad you stopped."

"Where are your band friends playing this weekend?"

"They're playing their last shows here tomorrow, Friday and Saturday nights at the Road House in Winona."

"Their *last* shows?"

"Yeah... then they're headed for New York."

"You going with them?"

"No... I'm staying here."

"So that's why you're looking a little lonely."

"Maybe."

"Well, my girlfriend is coming to visit this weekend. She's arriving tomorrow afternoon from Minneapolis. I came here to make plans with Francis and his wife to go out to dinner. Maybe we'll go to Winona, and then we can stop at the Road House for some good music and dancing. Will you be there?"

"Prob'ly... if the Knights don't decide to stay in Winona all weekend, like they did at Trempealeau."

"Great! Fischer said. "Then maybe we'll see you there."

"Sure! I'll be watching for you," I said.

"Okay. Well, Francis should be home by now. He's the resident engineer at the Genoa Dam project. You'll meet him tomorrow night, and I'm sure you'll like him... he's a great guy."

"Okay... see you tomorrow night."

I was glad that I had met Fischer. He was at least ten or twelve years my senior and his friend probably was, too. But what did it matter. We had a lot in common, and I was certainly interested in learning more about the new locks and dams on the river. He'd kept his word to look me up when he came to La Crosse, so I assumed that he was interested in building a friendship. And right now, it would be wise for me to make some new friends.

Soon after Fischer left, Luther strolled in looking hungry.

"Must be six-fifteen," I mused.

"Yeah, and I'm hungry."

We ordered our burgers and beer.

"The Knights are playing at the Road House in Winona tomorrow night," I said. "Wanna go?"

Luther pondered a long moment. "Are they there all weekend?"

I nodded.

"Well, then I'll go Friday or Saturday. I have to work Friday morning early, so I'd better not be out late tomorrow night. Don't wanna oversleep and be late for my last day of work at the hotel!"

Friday would be a work day for me, too, but I wanted to spend as much time as possible with Andy, Cheechee and Curtis, because I knew they'd be gone soon, and I didn't want to pass up the opportunity to nurture a budding new friendship with Fischer.

Just then, the Knights arrived after their late afternoon practice. They were hungry, too.

"Andy," I said. "Will you be staying in Winona overnight

tomorrow?"

"No, we're coming back here. "Why?"

"I'd like to go with you."

"Sure," he replied. "We'll have supper here, and we'll leave about seven-thirty."

Thursday was another sunny, hot day. Thundershowers were predicted for later that night, and the rain would certainly be welcome. But so far, the evening was still pleasantly warm and dry. After we ate our supper, we bid our farewells to Luther and headed to Winona, Minnesota in the shiny red Pontiac.

The Knights started their usual routine at nine o'clock— Andy and Curtis playing *Happy Days Are Here Again*, Cheechee jumping off the riser, wandering around the dance floor smiling, shaking hands, pouring on the charm—and as usual, the crowd loved it.

About ten o'clock I heard the thunder rumbling and saw the lightning flashes through the windows, and then the hiss of rain seemed to usher in a few gusts of cool, refreshing air. What a relief it was after so many hot, dry days.

A little while later, I waved to Fischer as he, his girlfriend, and another couple hustled in from the rain. By then there were no vacant tables, so we just stood off to the side and talked for a while. Fischer introduced his girlfriend, Marceline Patro, and his friends, Mr. and Mrs. Francis Landrieu. While the two women went off to the "powder room," Fischer, Francis and I talked about the much-needed rain. Francis wanted to know more about my riverboat background that Fischer had only briefly told him about. But then, the ladies came back and they wanted to dance. So our conversations after that were short and sometimes rather incomplete when the women dragged Fischer and Francis back on the dance floor as the Knights struck up another danceable tune. But we still had a good time.

The rain had diminished to merely sprinkles when I watched Fischer's 1932 Auburn sedan pull out of the parking lot. It was half past midnight, and I hoped Andy, Curtis and Cheechee wouldn't spend the rest of the night talking to someone again. I was tired, and I had to go to work in the morning. Fifteen minutes later, while I watched other people leaving, Curtis tapped me on the shoulder. "Ready to go?" he said, and then we dodged the few raindrops that were still falling.

A few miles south, the rain had stopped completely, but the road was wet and slick, so Curtis drove a little slower than usual. The storm had moved off to the east across the river; we could still see lightning bolts streaking through the distant clouds over Wisconsin.

There were no lights burning anywhere at La Crescent, just across the river from La Crosse. "Power must be out from the storm," Curtis said. His voice woke me; I had dozed off. Andy and Cheechee were sound asleep in the back seat.

As we approached the west end of the Mississippi Bridge at Pettibone Beach, Curtis slowed to a stop behind several other cars and what appeared to be a bus. I saw a lantern moving about in the darkness ahead, and then a man appeared. I judged him to be the bus driver by the hat he wore.

"What happened? Why are we stopped?" came sleepy voices from the back seat.

"I can't see anything," Curtis said. "Must be an accident."

We sat there for a few minutes without any movement of the traffic ahead. Then the man carrying the lantern came toward us. Curtis opened his door and got out. "The bridge has collapsed," I heard the man say. "You'll have to turn around... nothing can get through."

I could see the lights of La Crosse. We were so close. But I knew I wouldn't feel my pillow for a long time.

"We'll have to go back to Winona and cross the river there," Curtis said as he entered the car again.

"Why do you s'pose the bridge collapsed?" I asked.

"Prob'ly something with the storm," he replied.

Curtis turned his red Pontiac around in the road, as did the other drivers, and we all headed back to Winona. It was four o'clock when I laid my head down on my pillow.

CHAPTER FIFTY

MY ALARM CLOCK jarred me awake at seven. I guess it was my young stamina that allowed me to get out of bed, splash some cold water in my face, and attack the day. But I was still very tired.

"Did you hear about the bridge?" Larry, the night clerk asked as I passed by the front desk in the lobby.

"Huh? Oh, yeah," I said. "I was there... stranded on the other side at two o'clock this morning."

"Oh, so you know about the car that went down with it and the people drowned."

"No! I didn't know that. We turned around and went back to Winona... crossed the river there."

It was the buzz everywhere, and rumors sizzled like steaks on a grill. Uninformed reports were saying that a bus carrying thirty passengers had plunged into the river. I knew that wasn't true, because I saw the bus *and* its driver on solid ground. I thought it unlikely that he drove the bus off the end of the bridge after we left.

Later that day, when the afternoon paper hit the streets, I learned the shocking news. Even seeing it in print, I had difficulty believing it—Fischer Blinn had skidded and lost control of his 1932 Auburn sedan and crashed into the concrete and steel support girder, causing a 131-foot-long span of the bridge to collapse and plunge into the Mississippi River, taking the car with it. He escaped through the car window as soon as it hit the water, and then he had pulled his girlfriend out. He swam with the hysterical Miss Patro to the nearest shore pier where they were later picked up by a small police boat. The car had sunk in twelve feet of water; occupying the rear seat, Francis Landrieu and his wife had both suffered skull fractures in the crash and were unconscious, unable to help themselves. They drowned.

Fischer Blinn and Miss Patro were examined at St. Francis Hospital; no serious injuries were discovered other than severe shock.

Little had I known at two o'clock that morning that my new friend, Fischer and his girlfriend were clinging to a bridge pier, desperately struggling for their lives, and that Francis Landrieu and his wife had lost theirs—only a few hundred feet from where we sat curiously in the car. I was the last person to see them alive.

I never saw Fischer again.

CHAPTER FIFTY-ONE

TO SAY Monday August 12th, 1935 was a sad day in my life would be an understatement. While Fischer's accident was still heavy on my mind, Andy, Curtis and Cheechee had given me their official decision: they were going to New York. I realized that their choice held in store unlimited potential for their success as musicians; a multitude of opportunities as entertainers. But it also held in store danger and risk; I hoped they had counted those elements in their evaluation.

What made it a sad day for me, mostly, was that I would be parting company with my best friend of four years. Four years might not sound like a long time, but considering I ran away from home and all my friends and started life over only five and a half years ago, four years is a large portion. Andy had been the best friend anyone could have, and I knew I was gonna start missing him five minutes after he left.

Andy and I had breakfast together in the hotel dining room early that morning; Cheechee and Curtis were still sleeping. For over an hour we talked about our futures; I remained with a positive outlook on my job at the studio. The last thing I wanted was for Andy to be concerned about leaving me here alone. He was about to face plenty of his own concerns.

"Why don't you go back to St. Louis with Luther?" he asked.

"I'll tell you the same as I told Luther... I haven't thought of any good reasons to go back there... not right now."

Just then Cheechee and Curtis sat down with us. "G' morning, Will," they both greeted me. "Did we give you two enough time alone?"

"I guess so," I said.

"Are you sure you won't come with us?" Curtis pleaded. "It just won't seem the same without you."

I thought about all the good times the four of us had spent together... in St. Louis... traveling... in La Crosse... and for just one brief moment I was ready to pack my suitcase and venture out into the unknown. But then, just as quickly, reality set in, and the feeling of security with a sure thing put my clothes back in the bureau drawer. "Yeah, I'm sure," I said. "I think I've found my place in the world... and I think staying at the photo studio is the best choice for me right now."

"Well, we have a few things to do before we leave... get our money out of the bank, and get some traveling supplies, so if you change your mind in the next couple of hours..."

"I don't think I'll change my mind," I replied. "What time are you leaving? I'm going to work now, but I want to be here to see you off."

Curtis gazed at the big clock on the wall. "Ten o'clock... we should be ready to go by ten."

"Promise me that you won't leave 'til I get here."

"I promise."

I went to the studio and immediately told Mr. Jacob that my best friends were leaving town and that I needed a couple of hours off at ten o'clock.

"Take all the time you need," he said. "Where are they going?"

"New York," I replied. "I don't know when I'll ever see them again... if ever."

"Well, then... you'd better go say your goodbyes." He was so understanding; that was only one of the reasons why I liked working for him.

The shiny red Pontiac was parked at the curb, and Luther stood talking to the desk clerk when I returned to the hotel; Andy, Cheechee and Curtis stepped out of the elevator carrying luggage and a saxophone case. It was at that moment that their leaving seemed a reality. I had to fight back the tears.

As they approached the front desk, Luther said to the clerk, "I think I see a letter in their pigeon hole."

"Oh, yes," the clerk responded. "I almost forgot... it's for Andy Lorado." He retrieved the letter and handed it across the counter. With his free hand, Andy took the letter from him, folded it and stuck it in his hip pocket. "Thank you," he said.

"It's been a pleasure having you here," the clerk said. "Have a safe journey... and if you're in La Crosse again, please come and stay at the *Stoddard*."

Then we all walked across the lobby to the front door, out to the sidewalk, and I watched as the Knights piled their suitcases and the saxophone in the back seat. "You see?" I said. "There wouldn't have been room for all of us."

"We would have made room," Curtis said, and then he threw his arms around me and we hugged. "I'll miss you, Will," he said, sounding a little choked up. "I wish you were coming with us."

And then Cheechee took his turn for a tearful hug. "There's a notebook on the writing desk up in the room," he said. "I left it for you."

"Thanks, Cheechee," I said. "I hope you find a way to steal the stars in New York."

Andy was already wiping away the tears from his eyes. We embraced in a hug that I didn't want to end. "I'll miss you," he strained to say.

"Take good care of yourself," I said. My tears were streaming now, too.

"I'll write you a letter when we get..." He couldn't finish.

"Just remember me when you get rich and famous like Benny Goodman."

I watched them get in the car, and then the shiny red Pontiac slipped away around the corner.

A minute or so later, as I stood there alone staring at the street, I felt a hand on my shoulder. "I didn't just come here to talk to the desk clerk, you know," Luther said.

I wiped away tears from my cheeks. "Oh?" I replied.

He turned me toward the hotel entrance and guided me into the lobby. We sat in a couple of comfy chairs.

"I knew this would be a hard time for you," Luther said. "I thought I should be here with you."

"Thanks, Luther," I said. "Andy and I have been best friends for a long time... I miss him already."

"And I'm sure he'll miss you, too," Luther said. "But he has his career to pursue, and you have yours. Unfortunately, those careers aren't up the same road."

Luther was right. If for no other reason, I tried to make that the justification for Andy going to New York.

CHAPTER FIFTY-TWO

I MANAGED to get through the rest of the day at the studio. Because of the Mississippi River Bridge collapse, many amateur photographers had dropped off film they wanted Mr. Jacob to develop. So I had plenty to do that afternoon. But by five o'clock, I was eager and ready to go back to my room at the hotel. Emotional distress was setting in again, not only because of Andy's departure, but because in a couple of days, I would experience yet another loss of companionship—Luther would be leaving Wednesday, and there would be no one else left to help ease the pain.

When I passed the hotel front desk, the clerk hailed me. "Mr. Madison, sir," he said. "There is some mail here for you."

He handed me a letter. I immediately recognized the handwriting; it was from Sadie. "Thank you," I said, and headed for the elevator. "Third floor, Carl."

I studied the envelope in my hand, wondering why Sadie had written when, in fact, it was my turn to write to her. I squelched the urge to rip it open, right there in the elevator, and decided to wait for the privacy of my room.

Just as Cheechee had said, a notebook—the same notebook he gave me to read in St. Louis—lay on the writing desk. I flipped it open to discover many more pages had been written since I last saw it. Tucked between the pages was a note:

Dear Will,

You have been such a good friend. I haven't stolen any stars yet, but your inspiration has kept my story alive.

Your friend,

Christopher "Cheechee" Chapman

I wanted to sit right down, right then, and read Cheechee's continuation of *If I Could Steal the Stars*, but then I remembered Sadie's letter. That should be my first priority.

Sitting on the edge of the bed, I kicked off my shoes and then carefully tore open the envelope. Sadie usually had plenty to say, but this letter was astonishingly short:

Dear Will,

I hope all is well with you and the other boys.

I have some really good news for you. Jesse wants you to come back to St. Louis as soon as would be possible. He says your future employer would like to talk to you. I know you hate to leave your job there in La Crosse, but Jesse thinks you will be very pleased with what is waiting for you here.

Hope to see you soon.

Love,

Sadie

I checked the inside of the envelope to see if I had missed another page. It was extremely difficult to imagine that's all she would tell me! *My future employer wants to talk to me!* Suddenly my head was spinning with a hundred different thoughts all at once. Even though the letter was a bit mysterious, it could mean only one thing: Jesse must be the captain of his own boat now, and he is ready to get me back on the river! Yahoo!

I glanced at my watch. Ten minutes to six. I had time to relax in a bath before I met Luther for supper at the *Dixie of the North*.

At a quarter to seven, after the soothing bath, I felt as refreshed as if I had just slept for eight hours. I saw Luther already sitting at our usual table by the window in the *Bodega*. He waved as I walked by.

"You're looking mighty cheerful," he said when I sat down.

His comment reminded me of the events earlier that day. "I know I was almost in tears the last time you saw me—"

"Almost?" he said grinning.

"Okay. Maybe I *was*... and I'm still sad that Andy and the guys are gone. But I got a letter from Sadie today."

"And that made you happy again?"

I pulled the letter out of my shirt pocket and handed it across the table to Luther. "You read it and maybe you'll know why it makes me happy."

He unfolded the paper and read. A devilish little grin crept onto his face. He laid the letter on the table in front of me.

"So, when are you going to St. Louis?" he asked.

In all my ecstasy I had not yet thought about how and when. "I don't know," I said. "I'll hafta check... maybe the train..."

Luther held up his hand as if to stop me. He reached for his wallet, opened it, pulled out a green paper and handed it to me.

"What's this?" I asked.

"Look at it."

I unfolded the three-by-five inch card-like paper. It was a one-way ticket for a stateroom aboard the Passenger Steamer *St. Paul*, entitling occupancy by two persons; Departure time and date: 10:00 a. m., August 14, 1935 from La Crosse,

Wisconsin; Destination: St. Louis, Missouri.

Recollection of the "fare for two" came to me. Luther had told me of the tickets Spades gave him before he and Irene left. "So, I s'pose this means I'm going with you to St. Louis?" I said.

"It would be a shame to let the ticket go to waste," Luther replied.

Then it occurred to me. "The fourteenth is the day after tomorrow!"

"Yes it is," Luther said. "You have a whole day to get ready."

"Only one day," I whined. "But—"

"Let's eat," Luther said. "And then we can plan all the things you need to do. We'll have plenty of time... you'll see."

I was like a kite in a tornado. Lucky for me that Luther stayed there to hold onto the string.

CHAPTER FIFTY-THREE

IT SEEMED I was returning to St. Louis as abruptly as I had left, but for a better reason, and under much better circum-stances; I wouldn't have to be looking over my shoulder for pursuing police. Now that I knew the Tony Delaware case had been closed, I could rest easier.

Mr. Jacob didn't put up any fuss when I told him why my brother wanted me to come back to St. Louis, although I knew he was a little disappointed with my leaving. "You have to follow your heart," he said, "and if you find that your heart misled you to St. Louis, my door will still be open to you."

Follow my heart. That's what Spades Morgan had told me, too, and I desperately hoped that my heart wasn't leading me astray.

Lester Collins at the bank thought my returning to St. Louis—and Jesse—was a wise choice. He had always looked out for our best interests, and I had learned to trust his judgment. "You'd be like a mushroom out in the sunlight here all alone, Will," he told me. "Now that Andrew is gone, you *should* go back to your brother."

Lester withdrew all the money from my account for me, and after he had counted out $3,859.75 in cash, he reminded me of a safety precaution: "Get this cash into the ship's safe as soon as you board," he said. "You never know these days..."

"Thank you, Lester. You've been a great help."

"Say hello to Jesse and Sadie for me when you see them."

"I will, Lester. I will for sure."

Luther was like a little kid at a State Fair midway once we had boarded the *St. Paul*. I couldn't blame him—I was quite impressed, too. She was big and luxurious, and it was easy to see why Spades fancied this boat. Our stateroom was on the upper deck so we had a good view of the wrecked bridge as we passed through the open swing span. Construction crews were already at work on the temporary replacement span, but talk around town was that there would soon be a completely new, better bridge to connect La Crosse with Minnesota. For now, a ferry boat, called in from Prairie du Chien, was shuttling people and cars across the river.

The next four days seemed like a new adventure to me; even though I had travelled this river before, it had been so long ago. I remembered many of the towns we passed, because the Madison, unlike this much bigger boat, had stopped at nearly every one of them. But the hundreds of miles of shoreline were just vaguely familiar. It was a great experience, though, to ride as just a passenger, and to enjoy all the pleasures that the craft and crew provided.

There was plenty of time for me to read Cheechee's addition to his story. It continued with telling his experiences hitch-hiking across the country, enduring adverse weather conditions, begging for food when it was possible, stealing it when it was necessary. Then a miraculous ride with a trucker brought him the entire remaining distance to St. Louis.

When he arrived there, he decided to stay. His experience of living on the streets of Denver gave him the knowledge to live on the streets of St. Louis; he soon learned where the soup kitchens and bread lines kept him nourished.

Then he made some acquaintances that became good friends, and they took him in and helped him find a job. But his life in St. Louis was becoming a repeat of what he had left behind in Denver—until he met a couple of new friends named *Andy and Will.*

The story went on with a familiar ring, because now I had become part of his story. It continued with Cheechee's eloquent writing style, telling of his rise into entertainment, to our journey into Wisconsin, where perhaps he could *steal all the stars.*

Once again, I was quite impressed.

I had plenty of time, too, to imagine what new adventure awaited me. I could be nearly certain that I would finally see New Orleans, and perhaps the ocean. Jesse went there often, and so would I. But my imagination left me with so many unanswered questions, as I was sure Luther's imagination had him curious about Spades' new hotel. Trying to get anything more from him, though, was like trying to break into Fort Knox. I eventually gave up, and just watched the scenery go by, shooting a few pictures now and then, until we docked at St. Louis.

CHAPTER FIFTY-FOUR

THE ST. LOUIS SKYLINE was nothing new to me; I recalled my first arrival here and then it didn't seem so unusual that Luther appeared as if he were about to land on another planet. I had been wondering if anyone would be waiting at the levee for us; Luther assured me that Spades and Irene would be there. That seemed logical because Spades had purchased the tickets.

We stood at the railing on the upper deck, watching the St. Louis levee coming closer. Other passengers scurried by, toting bags, suitcases, and small children. Luther thought we should be among them.

"No hurry," I said. "The gangplank won't hit the ground for another fifteen minutes. There's already a mob of people gathered there... has been for the last half-hour."

"How do you know that?" Luther asked.

"I've seen it a thousand times," I replied.

"Oh, yeah. I suppose..."

As the huge craft gracefully floated to a stop, Luther raised his arm and pointed. "Look! There's Spades and Mom!"

I searched the crowd of people waiting in the hot sun on the levee. There they were, and beside them were Jesse and Sadie! What a pleasant surprise! Seeing them suddenly gave me the urge to hustle toward the gangplank. We retrieved our luggage from the stateroom and headed for the bow where a steward wished us a pleasant farewell.

My next pleasant surprise was seeing the rest of the welcoming party that had joined Spades and Jesse. Luke and Reggie were there, too, but my first priority was to receive one of Big Brother Jesse's bear hugs. I hadn't had one for months.

"Welcome home, Little Brother," Jesse whispered in my ear. Those were the most soothing words I had ever heard, not because I had returned to St. Louis, but because I had returned to my Big Brother.

Then there was a warm welcoming hug from Sadie. "I'm so glad you came back," she said. "You must've gotten my letter."

"Yes, I did," I said. "And just in the nick of time... another couple of days and I would've missed the boat."

"Good to have you back with us," Luke said, and then he and Reggie each gave me a hug.

I introduced Luther—who had been receiving an equally warm welcome from his mom and Spades. "He's been a great friend since the first day we arrived in La Crosse," I said.

"We've heard a lot about you from Spades," Luke said. "And we've been anxious to meet you." He and Luther shook hands, and then everyone else greeted him with sincere handshakes. Luther was already receiving acceptance, and in time, I knew everyone would like him as well as I did.

Luke and Reggie grabbed our luggage from the ground. "We'll take these to my car," Luke said.

"You have a car?" I said, a little surprised.

"Well sure! Didn't Sadie tell you in her letter?"

"I guess it slipped my mind," Sadie admitted.

After we had chatted for a while, and we had determined that everyone was in good health, Sadie excused herself; she had to go home because Philip's babysitter could only stay for a little while. Irene left with her.

Then Jesse commanded everyone's attention. I could easily tell that he was eager and anxious about something.

"Will," he said. "Shall we go see our new boat?"

This was the moment I had been anticipating for the last five days. He didn't have to ask twice. "Yes!" I responded instantly.

Shoulder to shoulder with Jesse we started down the levee; the others followed.

"Now, Will," Jesse said as we walked. "You know this won't be exactly the same as it was on the old Madison."

"Oh, I expected that much," I replied. "Are you and Luke captain and pilot?"

"We are."

"Will we be going to New Orleans?"

"Without a doubt."

After a hundred-yard walk, Jesse stopped me at the pointed bow of a freshly-painted blue and white, shined and polished, new-looking four deck excursion boat.

I gave Jesse a puzzled stare. I was expecting a squared bow with bumpers where the barges were attached. "This doesn't look like a barge towboat to me," I said.

"It's *not* a barge tow," he replied. By then, Spades was standing beside us. Jesse pointed to the front of the pilothouse; there, painted in gold and black letters was the boat's name, MADISON II. "Will?" Jesse said. "I'd like you to meet *our* new employer, Mr. Edward Morgan."

I glanced at Spades, and then quickly back to Jesse. He was grinning, and I suppose it was because of my utterly astonished expression. "Spades!" I said. "I thought you bought a hotel."

"You could say I did," Spades replied. "A *floating* hotel. Shall we go aboard for a tour?"

We stood on the bow admiring the beautifully-polished hardwood staircase that led to the next deck. "She's a very modern boat, Will," Jesse said. "Diesel power, propeller driven. No more coal shoveling, no more boiler fires, no more broken paddlewheel planks."

"Two hundred fifty feet long," Spades added. "Eighty staterooms, two dining rooms, two lounges, game room…"

I was in total awe. I couldn't believe my eyes. "And what's with the name?" I asked. I looked to Spades for the answer.

"Will," he said. "You and Jesse were my inspiration for undertaking such a project. I thought it was only fitting that my boat should be christened Madison II."

"Why didn't you tell me about it in La Crosse?"

"I couldn't. I had to get back to St. Louis first, and make sure Jesse would take command."

"He made me an offer I couldn't refuse," Jesse said smiling.

"So, how 'bout it, Will? Y'all gonna accept the position of the Official Photographer?"

"I… I…" I couldn't speak. I was standing on the main deck of the most attractive boat I had ever seen, my new adventure, and I couldn't utter a single word.

"Reggie will be my First Mate again," Jesse said. "Mildred and Beth will be the heads of housekeeping. I couldn't get Marion to leave his engineer job that he has, and I didn't think Lester would leave the bank in La Crosse, but I did find a few of our old deckhands. And I'm told that Luther will be an excellent steward."

I finally regained my composure. "Then our whole gang will be together again…" And then I remembered. "All except…" A lump formed in my throat. "All except Andy," I cried.

The next few moments were probably the most memorable ones of my entire life… for out of the shadows, down the pol-ished staircase came the sound of footsteps.

"Did I hear someone say my name?" a very familiar voice called out.

I spun toward the voice. Andy's beaming smile made every other sight and sound disappear into oblivion. Once again,

I became speechless.

"Hi, Dad," he said and gave a little wave. And then he gazed at me. "I was afraid you wouldn't make it."

I touched him to make sure he wasn't a mirage, and then we replayed the last hug at La Crosse. This time, it felt even better. Curtis and Cheechee took their turns, too.

"Did you know about this?" I asked when I came out of the clouds. Curtis and Cheechee smiled.

"Not until I remembered the letter from Dad that the desk clerk gave me just as we were leaving the *Stoddard*," Andy explained. "We were almost to Chicago. I forgot I had stuffed it in my pocket. I tried calling you on the telephone at the hotel that night, but Larry only said that you had checked out. He didn't know any more. So I could only hope that you went with Luther."

Curtis explained further. "We talked it over and we all agreed that New York was too far away... and the offer of House Band on a riverboat sounded more our style... you know, new audience every few days without having to go any-where."

"So we drove straight back to St. Louis," Cheechee added.

"You have no idea how glad I am that you didn't go to New York," I said.

Jesse and Spades gave me a full tour of our new boat, starting with the spacious main lounge, complete with stage, spotlights, and a glistening baby grand piano. Andy, Cheechee and Curtis stayed there with Luke, Reggie and Luther while my guided tour continued.

I saw the elegant staterooms, the magnificent galley and dining rooms, the recreation area, and the observation deck. We climbed more stairs to see the staff's quarters, laundry and utility rooms, and finally the largest and most comfortably furnished pilothouse I had ever seen. It looked more like a parlor... equipped with all the gauges, controls, and of course, the brass and teakwood steering wheel. I could easily understand why Jesse and Luke would never turn down this command.

While I was admiring all the exquisite appointments of the pilothouse, Reggie appeared at the door. "Luther wants to go to the *Dixie*," he said. "We're all going. Wanna come along?"

ABOUT THE AUTHOR

Born into a farm family in the late 1940s, J.L. Fredrick lived his youth in rural Western Wisconsin, a modest but comfortable life not far from the Mississippi River. His father was a farmer, and his mother, an elementary school teacher. He attended a one-room country school for his first seven years of education.

Wisconsin has been home all his life, with exception of a few years in Minnesota and Florida. After college in La Crosse, Wisconsin and a stint with Uncle Sam during the Viet Nam era, the next few years were unsettled as he explored and experimented with life's options. He entered into the transportation industry in 1975.

Since 2001 he has ten published novels to his credit, and one history volume, *Rivers, Roads, & Rails,* a non-fiction account of Midwestern history that focuses on the development of transportation during the pioneer days—steamboats, stagecoaches, and the beginnings of the Midwest's railroads— and the impact they had on the growth and prosperity of Midwest communities. He was a featured author during Grand Excursion 2004.

J.L. Fredrick currently resides at Poynette, Wisconsin.